WHEN THE WATER RUNS ØUT

DAVID CANFORD

Published by mad-books.com

7.24

Cover Design: Mary Ann Dujardin

To Megan, Toria and Millie

CHAPTER 1

The sound came out of nowhere. There was no build up. It went from silence to an intense buzzing, like some gargantuan insect in less than a second. When they heard it, they stopped walking and froze. They had been found. Only a few feet in front of them, a helicopter rose from below the top of the narrow mesa they were on.

"Run!" he shouted, turning and grabbing her by the arm.

The helicopter flew low above them. They felt the noise of it go through their bodies as they were buffeted by the tremendous wind its rotor blades created. Then it became quieter and the wind was gone just as quickly as it had arrived.

She was in front now. He tripped on a rock and fell. Sensing that he was no longer close behind her, she stopped to look but he was already on his feet again.

"Keep running!" he called. "It'll be back soon".

Ahead in the azure sky, the helicopter was already entering a tight turn to fly back toward them. The sun reflected off its fuselage, making it blinding to look at. They turned again to run away from it. Exactly where they could run to he didn't know. They were on a ridge in high desert country, exposed and with no hiding place in sight. But still they ran. It offered a mirage of hope rather than just standing and waiting to be obliterated.

The helicopter was closing on them now. He glanced behind him. It was higher this time. Something dropped from it, hitting the earth behind them. The ground beneath their feet reverberated like a massive earthquake, pieces of rock flying in all directions. Knocked off their feet by the force of the blast, they were catapulted off the edge.

Helplessly, they rolled down the steep slope toward the canyon floor below. By the time they arrived at the bottom, their clothes were shredded rags and bloodied from the cuts on their bodies. But they were alive, and at this point that was all that mattered.

The air was thick with falling dust. It was in their eyes and nostrils, even their mouths. It tasted gritty and unpleasant, however the dust gave them cover. A loud ringing from the deafening sound when the missile had exploded filled their ears.

He got up first. She tried to but fell over and let out a groan.

"I've done something to my foot."

"Here, put your arm around my shoulder," he said crouching down next to her.

They got up, she limping along by his side. He was extremely worried, the protection of the dust cloud was beginning to disappear. Escaping from the first attack had been a miracle. They wouldn't survive the next one. The unrelenting whirring of the helicopter would be the last thing they ever heard, its demonic outline the last thing which they ever saw.

They headed to where the canyon narrowed and rounded a corner. He had hoped to find a place of safety but a solid wall of rock more than one hundred feet high blocked their path. They were trapped. No way forward and no way back. The fear inside him rose to a new level. He fought hard to control the sense of mounting panic that would leave his mind paralyzed, unable to reason or function effectively.

He looked at the rock face. There seemed no obvious way to climb up it, and trying to do so would only make them a sitting target. If they went back, they would be walking into their own destruction.

He scanned their surroundings again and again. Then, to his right, he saw it. Their second miracle of the day. A small opening in the canyon wall, probably big enough for a human to squeeze through.

“Look! Over there.”

Helping her toward the opening, he pushed her into it just as the ominous buzzing sound returned, echoing through the canyon like the loudest sound system imaginable. He didn’t wait and quickly followed her.

But where was she, and where was he? The solid ground that he’d expected to be standing upon wasn’t there. He was falling, his arms and legs flailing. He heard a splash and then he too hit the water. The force of the impact hurt.

Despite the scorching temperature outside, the water was cold. His body plunged downward, the weight of his clothes dragging him ever deeper. At first, he was so surprised that he didn’t react. The water washed the thick layer of dust off him and felt refreshing, but as the pressure on his ears grew he realized that he would drown if he didn’t resist. With anxiety taking hold, he began to kick, kick upward. Initially, he continued to go down. Kicking harder, he at last began to rise. An overwhelming desire to breathe consumed him. Just when he thought he could hold his breath no longer, he broke through the surface.

It was hard to see. There was little visibility down here, only a small beam of light coming from the narrow gap through which they had entered, now out of reach and far above them. He could hear the sound of splashing.

"Are you all right?" he asked.

"Yeah, I think so."

"I'm gonna take your shoes off. They make it harder to swim." He went under the water. She shrieked with pain when he pulled the shoe off her injured foot. "Sorry," he said upon returning to the surface. "I completely forgot about your foot."

He removed his shoes too. As their eyes became accustomed to the poor light, they could see the extent of their predicament. They were inside an enormous underground chamber. He swam toward the sides, but there was no way they could get back up. The sides of the cave sloped diagonally, and there were no ledges to climb out onto. They were stuck in deep water, getting colder by the minute.

After all they had been through, is this how it would end, dying of exhaustion and hypothermia in a place which no one knew existed? How ironic that out here in the desert they should find themselves trapped by water.

"I don't think I can keep this up much longer," she said as she continued treading water.

He looked around, peering into the dimness, scouring their surroundings for a passage out of this watery prison. At one point the wall of the cave was undercut. Beneath it a small space, maybe a foot high above the water. Did it lead somewhere?

He swam across and into the undercut, pushing his hands against the roof of it to make progress. Within a few feet, the roof sloped down under the water. As he sank beneath the surface, total darkness enveloped him. His heart rate tripled. He swam further on. Reaching out with his hands, he could touch the sides. After a short distance, it had become so narrow that he couldn't turn around. Retreating backward until the tunnel widened, he swam back to where she was waiting.

"Did you find a way out?" There was a note of hope in her voice, an unspoken wish to be told that they were going to get out of here.

"I can't tell for certain. One thing's for sure, if we stay here we won't survive. We don't have a choice. We've got to at least try."

She said nothing and didn't move. He tried to encourage her. "Come on, this way." He began to swim but she didn't so he swam back to her.

"Don't give up now, we can make it."

"I know that," she said but she still didn't budge.

"Look, I'm frightened too but I'm more afraid of doing nothing."

"How will I know where you are?"

"It's a narrow tunnel. We can't lose each other." They swam to the undercut. "Let's rest here a moment and get our breath back."

Both their hearts continued thumping even when they had rested, beating with trepidation. Was there a way through? Could they reach it? If not, would they have gone too far to get back before they drowned? There was no way of knowing.

"Let's do this," she said.

Edging forward to where the roof of the undercut sloped down into the water, they both took a deep breath and went under; he in front, she just behind him. Their arms and legs soon began bumping the sides of the narrow tunnel. As they went on, the seconds ticked by. They had gone too far now to get back before they ran out of what little breath they had left. Up ahead it was still dark, no sign of this underwater tunnel coming to an end. They could feel water in their nostrils. Each of them fought the desire to breathe. How they wanted to but all they would feel would be the cold, lifeless water that would make them convulse and gasp as their lungs filled with liquid while they died. The urge to inhale was fast becoming irresistible.

In desperation, he rose up. His head hit the rock ceiling, but he could sense that he had broken through the surface. A small gap between the solid rock above them and the water. He flipped his body over to get his nose and mouth into the tiny space and breathe. Reaching down for her arm, he pulled her up. They stayed there for a couple of minutes getting their breath back, spreadeagled on their backs with their legs and arms pressed against the sides to hold themselves in position, their faces up against the hard, unyielding rock.

"Are you okay to go on?"

"I guess so," she replied without conviction.

They drew their limbs into their sides, sank under the water again and rolled over so that they could move forward. After only a short distance, he saw a faint glimmer in the water ahead. The tunnel widened as they swam on. They broke through the surface. They'd done it!

They had arrived in another chamber. This one was much brighter; a large beam of sunlight shone in at an angle from the world above like in a religious painting. There were rock ledges which they could access. Swimming toward the one nearest them, they gratefully clambered onto it.

Smiling at each other, they gulped oxygen, exhausted from their ordeal but glad to be alive. They were saved, or were they? Yes, they were on dry land and no longer in freezing water quickly losing their body heat, but they were still underground with no visible way to climb up and out. The cave walls were vertical. They remained trapped. No one could hear them or knew that they were here.

After a few minutes, he slid back into the water and swam around the cave, searching for a way through to another one, but there were no exits other than from where they had just come. He didn't have to say anything when he returned to the ledge. She knew. Neither said anything. What was there to say? He shuffled across the ledge to be close to her and put his arm around her. She buried her face in his chest.

They had come so far and got so close to succeeding.

CHAPTER 2

Thirty-thousand feet below, the shadow of Air Force One crossed yet another lake. Seated by a window, the President looked down upon the vast wilderness of water and forest below. There were no roads, no signs of human habitation. They'd been flying across this landscape for three hours now, yet still it continued with no end in sight.

He had never flown across northern Canada before, or if he had he hadn't noticed. His flights back to Washington from Europe had always been farther south. On this occasion, he was flying straight from a G20 summit in London to Las Vegas to join his buddies, the "South Wasters", as he liked to call the governors of California, Arizona, and Nevada in jest, for a game of golf and some election strategy.

The summit had been interminable and boring, endless photo sessions and meaningless communiqués. It was worse than a large family gathering with all those relatives who you had nothing in common with but were obligated to meet up with once a year. He'd certainly earned the right to this golf trip.

Ted Jackson was tall and slim, an urbane man with a shock of thick, prematurely gray hair and engaging brown eyes. When he turned on the charm, he had an appealing smile, but he also had a determined, ruthless streak, as anyone who wanted to reach his position needed to have.

Jackson became interested in politics when only a teenager. It was then that his father had suffered the double misfortune of losing his job and falling severely ill in quick succession. No longer employed, he and his family had no health insurance. The medical bills had bankrupted his mom and dad. They'd lost their comfortable home in the Queen Anne neighborhood of Seattle and found themselves living in an RV which a friend had loaned them. The experience had made him question why, in the richest nation on earth, so many didn't have healthcare, leading him to become an activist for the Democrats.

In his late twenties, he'd given up a successful law career to enter politics full time. Jackson was a fighter. He'd had to fight hard to win his first term and would fight tooth and nail to win a second term next November. No President wanted to be remembered for being a one-term President. However, things were finely balanced. His party had lost control of Congress in the midterm elections last year. Jackson had recovered in the polls since then, but one major mishap could dash his chances of reelection. California and the Southwest would be a crucial battleground, and he needed his golf buddies to help raise the campaign finance to keep those States.

The captain appeared.

"Where are we?"

"Over northern Saskatchewan, Canada, sir."

"I've never seen so many lakes."

"Yeah, they sure have a lot of them. It's three hours to Vegas, sir."

"Guess I better get the team together and do some work, then."

Jackson got up and walked into the adjacent section of the plane to talk with his staff.

Exactly three hours later, Air Force One touched down in Las Vegas. As always, for security reasons, it came to a halt with the side of the aircraft where the President was sitting facing away from the terminal. A few minutes later and already in his golf gear, he half walked and half ran down the stairs with a bounce in his step into the waiting limousine, the cares of office briefly forgotten.

That evening, the four men sat around a table in a private room in the Wynn Hotel drinking cold beer straight from the bottle, refreshed from an afternoon on the golf course and satisfied from the excellent burger and fries served by special request. Jackson had had his fill of haute cuisine at the G20. He'd craved something good and simple, something American, not that pretentious European food which left you still feeling hungry. When they finished eating, they dismissed the waiters.

"So, my South Wasters, when are you all going to come to DC so I can whip your asses on the golf course?"

"Whip our asses? Haven't you got that the wrong way around? Who was fumbling with his balls in the rough half the afternoon?" joked Seth Baldwin, the African American governor of California. Stocky and powerfully built, the man had enjoyed a successful career in football when younger.

The others laughed. It was good to be in the company of friends, thought Jackson. It had been a perfect day.

"Guys, I'm sorry to put a downer on things but there's an issue we need to bring you in on, Ted," said Carlos Jimenez, the Latino governor of Arizona. He wasn't tall and photogenic like Ted. His face was badly pockmarked from acne but his hair remained black. Despite his love of burritos, chimichangas, and all Mexican cuisine, he had only a moderate middle-aged paunch.

"Jeez, Carlos, that sounds mighty serious," sighed Jackson. "I was really hoping to enjoy just one problem-free evening."

"It is serious I'm afraid, extremely serious in fact. You know that we already have a severe water shortage here in the Southwest. Well, we've just received data that we could literally run out of the stuff in a couple of years, maybe less, without drastic cutbacks that would end life here as we know it."

"What do you mean? You can't run out of water that fast. I knew there was an issue but it was much more long term than that," said Jackson, a genuine concern in his voice.

"We thought so too, but it seems the information we had was plain wrong. Without a massive reduction in consumption which would tank the economy, we're told water supplies will simply run out."

"You're messing with me."

Jackson laughed but it was a hollow laugh. The media and the Republicans would play it as his fault, his failure for not having taken action to deal with one of the greatest threats facing the country. This would undoubtedly cost him next year's election unless he could turn it around.

Although he was shocked by the news, it shouldn't have come as a surprise. The reality is southern California and the Southwest are one big desert. A magnificent desert but a desert nonetheless, never meant to support the millions who live there. A vast and impressive land of deep canyons, high mesas, and rugged mountains, all dominated by one thing: aridity. In its cities existed illusion, green lawns and spectacular fountains. It had been desert before the Europeans arrived and it remained so despite man's ingenuity in having made it habitable.

For centuries, it had been only sparsely populated by Native Americans. Moving north from Mexico, the Spanish gradually established a tenuous foothold, building presidios and missions. In the 1840s, the United States waged a successful war against Mexico, acquiring a vast new territory including Texas, the Southwest, and California. However, the number of inhabitants remained small.

After World War Two, the region's population began to grow exponentially. People were drawn by the climate and job opportunities. For decades, the residents had been using up the limited water supplies much faster than they could ever be replenished by nature. Everyone knew there was insufficient water but preferred to ignore the problem, because to deal with it would mean unpalatable changes to their way of living. After years of severe drought, the future had become the present all too soon.

"I wish we were just messing with you, Ted," said Carl Olsen, the rotund and burly governor of Nevada. "But it's as real as the pimples on my ass. Lake Mead is emptying faster than a bathtub. Once it and Lake Powell get too low, the aqueducts to LA and San Diego will dry up. And we're all fighting amongst ourselves about who gets what little we have. In the last few years, the snow line in the Rockies has moved ever higher. The snowmelt we rely on is a fraction of what it was, so the Colorado ain't half the river it used to be. We need your help, we can't fix thison our own. It's way too big for us to deal with."

"How do you know the data is correct?"

"Oh believe us, Ted, we've been through that loop many times. We've had it confirmed and re-confirmed."

"Then why the hell wasn't it picked up before?"

"We don't know," said Seth. "The earthquake last fall didn't help. We never told folks the whole story to avoid panic, but it created underground fissures and saltwater is fast leaking into the Sacramento - San Joaquin delta. It's responsible for two-thirds of my state's water so a severe reduction in supplies from there to Southern California is inevitable. And most aquifers are close to exhaustion from over extraction. On top of all that, it seems we could be facing a mega drought - one which could last twenty or thirty years. Apparently, California had them back in the twelfth and thirteenth centuries. Scientists have worked it out from looking at tree rings but back then it wasn't a problem, the population was only a few thousand."

"Have you come up with any solutions?"

"None that the voters would accept. We've already got many conservation measures in force which are mighty unpopular. If we cut everyone's water consumption by ninety per cent, we'd buy ourselves a few years to do something but it would be political suicide. Can you imagine shutting down California's agriculture? That's only one of the many unpalatable things we'd need to do."

No, Jackson couldn't imagine doing that. California had everything needed to be the perfect land for agriculture except rain, so massive water transfer infrastructure had been constructed last century. Half the nation's fruit and vegetables were grown there as well as it being the country's leading dairy producer. All this required prodigious amounts of water, more than nature could sustain.

“Okay fellas,” said Jackson, still reeling from the evening’s revelation but already moving into action mode. “I’ll get straight on it. How many people know about the extent of the problem?”

“Very few,” answered Carlos. “A handful of state employees bound to secrecy, and none of them really has a complete picture. Only we three and a few trusted advisers have access to all the pieces of the jigsaw puzzle.”

“Good, well make sure it stays that way until we have a solution, and even then it might be too sensitive to share with the nation. You boys sure know how to spoil a good evening. I was going to spend the night here, but I need to get back to the White House. I need to meet with my people first thing tomorrow. Send me a copy of the data so I can have it analyzed overnight.”

Within an hour, Air Force One was airborne heading east through the night for the capital, the cabin lights dimmed. In his private cabin at the front of the aircraft, the President was tense and restless. This was going to be the biggest challenge of his Presidency. If he handled it correctly he would be remembered as a great President, but if he blew it he would forever be remembered as the President who failed to save California and the Southwest.

He called through to the main cabin and asked Julia, his favorite intern, to come through.

"Lock the door after you," he said as she entered.

Julia was an attractive brunette, curvaceous and womanly, not one of the usual stick insects. It was a high-risk game, but he was a man who got a thrill from taking risks.

CHAPTER 3

Angel Tarak had felt free as he left the city of Phoenix behind him earlier that same day and headed east in his pickup toward the Superstition Mountains. He loved the open space and communing with nature. The excitement it gave him surged through his whole being.

The sky was beginning to lighten and soon the sun would rise. Angel had started out before six, wanting to take advantage of the relative cool of dawn. With a hot wind predicted, the temperature today would be well in excess of one hundred degrees in the shade.

Angel had adopted Tarak, an Apache name meaning star, as his last name when he became eighteen. His father had been an Apache. Apaches have no last names, and Tarak had been his father's first and only name.

Angel wore his black hair down to his shoulders, and a wide band of red cloth around his head. His face was round, his jaw square. His eyes, like many Apache, naturally appeared bloodshot, which is why they had named the white man “white eyes”.

A prominent scar ran at forty-five degrees across the left cheek of his face, acquired in a knife fight as a teenager. Born with a fiery temper, he had always retaliated when other kids taunted him with “Hey Tonto” and other derogatory terms. In police custody many times, he’d only recently been released from a year in jail for assaulting a guy in a bar who had unwisely told him to “fuck off back to your tipi”.

Angel had no memories of his father, who’d been shot trying to rob a gas station when Angel was only a baby. His fondest childhood memories were of visiting his Apache grandmother on the San Carlos reservation in southeastern Arizona. He went there until he was twelve when she too had died. Angel cherished his Apache heritage and yearned to be part of their culture, but he no longer had any contact with those who lived on the reservation.

His grandmother had instilled in him a strong sense of where he came from. She’d educated him in the ways of their forebears, teaching him how to survive in this harsh land. She hadn’t been your typical grandmother, not warm and cuddly, soft and soothing. Her skin was wrinkled from a life in the hot sun. Her hands were like sandpaper and she smelled earthy. Although she had been probably only sixty at most, she looked much older. To a young child, as Angel then was, she seemed positively ancient, an impression reinforced by her almost total lack of teeth.

She drove Angel relentlessly to learn the valuable skills and endurance of his ancestors, pushing him to his limits and sometimes beyond. If his feet were sore and blistered from running for many miles she, accompanying him bareback on her horse, ignored his complaints, cajoling and goading him to go further. By the age of ten he was already bigger than this diminutive figure, but she had a force of personality that no one who encountered her could ignore.

If Angel was hungry, she left him to find his own food. She rarely helped him out if he struggled, but he'd loved her deeply. He thrived under her tutelage and remained grateful to this day that she had taught him how to survive out here, skills that few of today's residents of the Southwest possess. They never imagined for one moment that they might have to live without the comforts of twenty-first century life which allowed them to forget how precarious human existence in this region really was.

His grandmother had shown him how to make a wickiup, the traditional domed round shelter used by the Apache, from desert broom, and thatch it with bear grass, and how to find food in this barren land which most could not see. He'd learned to survive on agave and prickly pear, and to make soap and shampoo from the root of the yucca plant. She had also shown him how to use the agave as a form of string by cutting it correctly and pulling out fibers from the fleshy leaf with the sharp pointed end of the leaf still attached, which made the perfect needle and thread to repair his moccasins when they wore out.

Under her guidance, Angel also learned how to hide and not be found. The Apache were masters of concealment. Above all, she'd drilled into him the importance of resilience.

After a day of stretching him to the limit, she would reward him with tales of their people's past. She would delight her grandson with stories of how he was descended from Goyakla's band of warriors, perhaps the most famous Native American leader of all, known to the white man as Geronimo.

Required to live on the reservation at San Carlos where conditions were bad, a group led by Geronimo fled into the mountains of Mexico. He had a particular reason to hate the Mexicans. They had murdered his mother, wife, and children, throwing the youngest in the air and impaling them on bayonets. Geronimo took his revenge upon many, torturing and killing without mercy or hesitation.

Eventually, thanks to Apache scouts, the army found Geronimo and his followers, and he agreed to return and live on the reservation. "Once I moved about like the wind. Now I surrender to you and that is all," were his words of capitulation.

Permitted to travel back separately from the army, a rogue agent, worried at his loss of lucrative business if the war ended, told them the soldiers planned to kill them. Geronimo and a small band fled back to Mexico from where they conducted many daring raids into the United States. It took five thousand soldiers, a quarter of the US army at that time, helped by Mexican troops and scouts, many months to find Geronimo and his contingent of only thirty-four, including women and children, in the Sierra Madre mountains.

Assured that they would be reunited with their families and spend only a short time in exile, they agreed to surrender. Clapped in chains, the Apache were sent in a windowless train to Florida never to return. Even the Apache scouts who had helped track down Geronimo were exiled. For many years the men were imprisoned, and their children were sent to school hundreds of miles away from their parents. It marked the end of Native American resistance, but Geronimo remains an evocative character of defiance even today.

As a boy, Angel would relive the tales of the warriors' guerrilla war his grandmother recounted, tracking wildlife and pretending they were the enemy. He would imagine himself as a modern day Geronimo, taking up arms for his people and recovering their land. Proclaimed a hero, he would be compared to the great Apache leaders of the past.

To Angel, like Geronimo, Arizona was more than home, it was a magical, life-giving place, though much of the state had now, in his opinion, been desecrated by the voracious demands of the millions who'd come here to claim their place in the sun. Where once there had been awe and wonder, and night skies filled with more stars than you could possibly count, neon lighting hid their beauty and the living earth suffocated under mile upon mile of suburban sprawl and bumper to bumper traffic.

As Angel saw it, what had taken millions of years for the elements to create, had been made sterile in little more than a hundred years.

Arizona suffered huge environmental damage when the settlers arrived. Overgrazing by their cattle destroyed the grass that once protected the land and nature's delicate balance. Without that grass, the occasional rain which fell was no longer absorbed. It ran off along arroyos in muddy torrents until it was so thinly spread it evaporated, nourishing little.

However, due to the state's size, its challenging climate, and limited water resources there remained large areas not yet bulldozed into suburbs and strip malls. It was to those places Angel came whenever he could.

Angel turned onto a dirt track, and after a few miles pulled over. He grabbed his backpack and walked toward what appeared to be a sheer rock face, but which he knew hid a steep path amongst the rocks that would lead him to the top and a panoramic view across open country. Initially, his route took him past magnificent saguaro cacti, an iconic emblem of the region, many shot full of bullet holes by those with no respect for the natural world.

While he ascended, he drank regularly. Dehydration was all too easy to fall victim to out here. After a couple of hours, he pulled himself up over rocks blocking the last few feet to his destination, a flat space about one hundred feet by fifty, backed by further rock faces on two sides. Angel stood smiling at the incredible view. How he loved it out here, it made his heart sing. He walked to the northern edge. A sheer drop of over a thousand feet lay below. On the horizon stood more mountains, their primeval volcanic ridges sentinels to this wonderful place.

He sat down dangling his legs over the edge, took off his backpack, and got out a chicken wrap he'd bought on his drive here. The sun now high in the sky warmed him. The temperature was hot but not stifling as at lower altitude. For a long time he remained there, soaking in the vista and the silence.

A low growling behind him interrupted his reverie. Angel's heart rate quickened. Getting up, he removed his handgun from its holster. Only twenty feet away from him, and staring at him intently, stood the most awesome of creatures with its powerful, muscular forequarters supported by large paws. Its jaws opened, revealing its pink tongue and powerful teeth with the characteristic long canines at either side perfectly crafted by mother nature to bite into and crush the skull of its prey. About three feet tall, its coat tawny in color, it was a mountain lion, the most fearsome predator in the Southwest.

Angel had never seen one before other than in a zoo. Secretive creatures, generally out hunting only at dawn or dusk, they usually avoided humans unless they felt threatened. Angel didn't understand how he could have made the animal feel in danger. He knew that he should back away slowly but he couldn't. He was on a cliff edge. Standing as tall as he could, he began shouting at the creature. Angel wanted to reach down for rocks to throw at it, but it could leap across the space between them in an instant. He also understood that if he fired his gun and missed, it could be on top of him pinning him down with its claws and biting with immense force before he got a second chance.

Angel's heart was thumping and his pulse raced. Cold sweat trickled from under his arms and down his body. The mountain lion drew back slightly and crouched down and hissed. It was going to attack. Angel fought to keep his cool. He would have only one chance of survival. It leaped high into the air as it flew toward him, claws extended, traveling at lightning speed and with incredible grace. A wondrous sight but a vision of death.

As the mountain lion fell through the air toward him, Angel fired his gun. The weight of its body knocked Angel onto his back. But he was lucky, his bullet had penetrated the creature's heart. He felt it become lifeless while he lay there with his upper body leaning backward over the ledge, the mountain lion's corpse on top of him, its face pressed against his. Warm saliva from the beast dribbled onto Angel's face. Ironically, its coat felt soft and comforting, and its whiskers tickled his cheeks.

With some difficulty he removed the mountain lion's claws, which had pierced the skin on his shoulders and wriggled out from under it. Angel pulled its body back onto the ledge and sat down next to it, shaken from the ordeal. It was a humbling reminder of how tenuous life can be. His t-shirt was wet with blood from the animal.

Although he had come close to death, Angel regretted having to kill this magnificent beast. He remained where he was for a while, recovering from the shock of the incident before gathering his belongings and heading over to the steep path down.

Turning around for one last look as he was about to disappear below the rim, Angel was astonished to see a small cub scamper from its hiding place behind a rock to its dead mother and try to suckle. Now Angel understood why he'd been attacked. The mother had thought him a threat to her young. He climbed back up and walked over to where the cub had appeared from. There was no sign of any other cubs. Although a mountain lion might have as many as six cubs in a litter, though more typically just two, usually only one survives.

This cub would die too if Angel left it here. He went across to it and gathered it in his arms.

The cub didn't resist, seeming to sense that Angel wouldn't hurt it. The size of a small cat, its coat was a darkish brown with spots and spiky in appearance, not much more than a ball of crazy fur. It nuzzled against him, vulnerable and defenseless.

Angel gently put the cub in his backpack so it could see out but not escape and began to descend. He would take it to the zoo in Phoenix where it could be cared for. Maybe they would have a conservation program and the cub might one day be released back into the wild. Angel hoped for that; this creature belonged out here where it was free to roam and live in dignity, not in some cage. To an Apache being confined was worse than death, to them it was better to die than be incarcerated.

CHAPTER 4

The President was back in the Oval Office by seven. At eight Ann Jones, the Secretary of State and Chip O'Hara, the Secretary of Defense, arrived. Ted got up from behind his desk in front of the bay windows, his hand outstretched toward the two couches facing each other.

"Thanks for clearing your schedules and getting here so early guys," he said sitting down on the sofa opposite them.

"That's no problem. We're keen to know the reason, though. You don't normally call a meeting this early, so we're guessing it's something pretty serious," said Ann.

Ann was about fifty, of average height with a silver bob. Her charcoal business suit complimented her green eyes. She'd made her fortune in the family business which her father had started, a natural resources conglomerate. Her business deals meant that she was on first name terms with a number of the world's despots, which had proved invaluable on many foreign policy issues since her appointment almost three years ago.

"It is serious. I met up with the Southwestern governors yesterday and it seems that our data on water resources is inaccurate. Long story short: Southern California, Arizona, and Nevada will run out of water within a couple of years. The dams, the rivers, and the aquifers will all be exhausted from overuse."

For a few moments complete silence reigned while Ann and Chip processed this information.

"But that's not possible," said Chip, a short, bald man with pebble-thick glasses, wearing a suit a size too big for his small frame. Despite the initial impression that might be given by his appearance, he was a tough and effective operator well respected by those he worked with.

"I'm afraid it's a cold, hard fact. I couldn't believe it either but I've had the data verified. I want us to move on this, and move on it fast. Water is the most vital resource of all. It seems the NSA reported as long ago as the 1970s that the biggest long-term threat to our economy was the lack of fresh water resources in California and the Southwest. But the problem's never been dealt with. And now we've reached the end of the road and we're staring into the abyss.

"We're talking about nothing less than a

dangerous threat to our national security, but I need it kept under the radar. If this gets out, there'll be panic and an economic crisis. An area accounting for over fifteen percent of our economy will cease to be viable in only two years' time. You can imagine how it would play out politically. I need you to present me with solutions here tomorrow at the same time. I want you to involve only those who you can really trust. This information is dynamite. We can't deal with the problem in the glare of publicity."

"That's really not much time," protested Ann.

"It's not but time is one thing we don't have."

He stood up to indicate the meeting was over.

"I sure didn't see that one coming," said Ann in the corridor outside the Oval office.

"Me neither," agreed Chip. "It looks like our people will be pulling another all-nighter."

The USA has been running out of water for years. The Ogallala aquifer, a vast underground water system on which the agriculture of the Great Plains depends, is being depleted fourteen times faster than it can be replenished by nature and could be exhausted by 2050. In the Southwest, the Colorado river, the lifeblood of that region, has already been strained to its limit, not to mention the Rio Grande which brings water to New Mexico and Texas. Underground sources, which take many thousands of years to refill, have in many places been over-exploited to the point of exhaustion.

The USA's water consumption, which is more per person than any other nation, has hastened the problem. Without adequate water supplies, Southern California and the Southwest would revert to an empty place, and result in the biggest forced migration in history.

Nations have fretted often about oil running out and fought wars to obtain and protect their supplies, but the liquid gold of this century is water. There is simply not enough of it to meet the needs of the world's population. Many have predicted that the wars of the future will be about water.

The next morning, they reconvened in the Oval Office. Ann and Chip sat down on a sofa while the President paced back and forth, agitated.

"Tell me what you've come up with."

"This is a difficult assignment," said Chip. "There's no more fresh water today than when the dinosaurs roamed the earth. The amount available doesn't change. What they peed is the same water we're drinking today. It falls as rain, gets used, and is evaporated back up to fall as rain again. But with climate change, California and the Southwest are getting even drier-"

"I want solutions, not a lecture."

"There's no easy answer. Shipping water from Alaska would help a little, but there simply aren't enough ships. It's a band-aid at best. The Great Lakes are already shrinking and polluted, and one day soon you're going to need to look at taking water from them, despite the protests that will unleash, to help the Midwest cope with its own water shortages and the pollution to existing water supplies caused by all that fracking your predecessor was so keen on. Our team looked at the possibility of diverting water from the Mississippi, but that too would interfere with shipping, and would be opposed by those states the river runs through."

"And the Northwest? I grew up in Seattle. It rains a lot there, believe me. They must have water to spare."

"We considered the Columbia river that flows through Oregon too," answered Chip. "But it's been contaminated by nuclear waste from Hanford leaking into the water system. And the folk up there aren't going to agree to water transfer. Don't Californicate Oregon is their mantra. The bottom line is any solution from our own limited resources will stir up protest and legal challenge. We would get nowhere in the time we've got, and it would all be under an intense media spotlight."

"Exactly," agreed Ann.

"What about desalination plants?" asked Ted. "They already have some in California."

"That's a good question, sir. I'd forgotten to mention them," replied Chip. "I had the exact same thought. It seems they're not the panacea you might think. Not only are they extremely energy intensive but they damage marine ecosystems by sucking up plankton, and the process leaves a toxic brine which increases salinity making the conversion to usable water even harder. We would also be talking about a huge scale here. In my opinion, it would cost you California next fall. The beautiful people of Southern California would not thank you for taking away their beach front and replacing it with desalination plants."

"So what's the answer then?"

"It seems there is only one," said Ann.

"And what's that?" Jackson's tone betrayed his frustration at the time this was taking.

"Canada. They have the water we need, and they're never going to use it themselves.

They have less than one percent of the world's population but a tenth of its freshwater. The problem is it would be political suicide for the Canadian government to give it to us. You know what they're like up there. We're the big, bad wolf just waiting to grab their resources."

"That's why it has to stay out of the public eye, at least until it's got beyond the point of no return. What are you proposing?"

"Let me show you."

Ann projected a 3D image from her device into the space in front of them. The President stopped pacing and stood behind her, hands on the sofa leaning forward to see. A map of North America appeared.

"What do you know about the Northwest Territories?"

"The Mountie always gets his man?"

Ann ignored his attempt at humor and changed the image to a map of the area.

"Choosing something near the border would get noticed too easily, but way up there no one need know for a long time. The lakes are so big that it could be years until anyone knew what was happening. The Northwest Territories are nearly three times the size of California with a population of less than fifty-thousand people.

We are talking wilderness with a capital W. Those two large blue areas are Great Bear Lake and Great Slave Lake, both in the top ten largest lakes in the world, they're huge. They contain enough water to fill Lake Mead over a hundred and fifty times. Right now the water in them drains into the Arctic Ocean."

Jackson appreciated her intellect. Ann was an excellent expositor with an incredible head for detail.

"And just how do we get it down to the Southwest?"

"A pipeline, well a few of them to be exact," answered Chip.

Ann obligingly changed the image in front of them to one showing a proposed route from the lakes in Canada down to the Colorado river.

"Timescale?"

"If you're willing to order the military to assign the resources we could have it built in time, and it would be a huge boost to our industry also," said Chip.

"Won't the water freeze in the pipes? It has to be at least twenty below up there for half the year?"

"We have the technology to deal with that – insulation, heating in the pipe, all that stuff. It's a challenge but we can do it. There'll still need to be some serious reduction in consumption but we wouldn't be talking watergeddon anymore."

"And the cost? Billions, I guess."

"Yes, but as Benjamin Franklin said, 'When the well's dry, we know the worth of water'. We have some wiggle room in the defense budget, and I'm thinking you could get us some more money from elsewhere for something this important."

"Okay, let's do it. The cost of not doing it would be worse. And Ann, I want you in Ottawa tomorrow. Your job is to convince the Canadian Prime Minister to buy this. Their economy is reliant on access to ours. You can play that card. Chip, I want the Pentagon to plan how to take it by force if Ann's diplomacy doesn't work."

"But, Mr. President," said Ann, "Canada's an ally, a very close ally."

"That's exactly why they should help us, that's what you're supposed to do for a friend. I'm not going to abandon California and the Southwest, or my next term if they won't help us. I'll talk to the governors about implementing extra conservation measures."

But the President had no intention of doing that. Cutting back consumption on anything more than a minor scale wouldn't win him any votes next November. He had already decided that meaningful reductions in water usage could be delayed until after the election.

"I appreciate you guys getting on top of this so quickly. Chip, I need you to report to me as soon as possible with a plan of how we make this happen if our request is refused by the Canadians. And Ann, call me from Ottawa after your meeting."

"Mr. President you're going to need Canada's co-operation. They're not some third world country we can just kick around."

"Ann, that's exactly why I chose you to be my Secretary of State. You can persuade anyone to do anything."

"Well, we'll have to see about that," she said standing to go and walking toward the door.

"You know you can. I have every confidence in you," the President called after her.

CHAPTER 5

Mingan enjoyed watching his birchbark canoe glide across the surface of the water. Barely disturbing it, the bow carved through a perfect reflection of the sky and clouds above. Silently crossing the lake, all signs of the canoe's passing quickly vanished.

Mingan had crafted the canoe himself. Birchbark was the perfect material. Water-resistant and cardboard-like, it could be easily bent and sewn. His ancestors had used it for thousands of years to build canoes to travel across this vast land.

How pristine was his world, thought Mingan. He felt fortunate to have been born in this place when so many had to live shut away from the natural world, observing life through a prison of glass. Be it through their car windshield while stuck in traffic, or the window of their office, or their apartment overlooking other buildings. Did those urban dwellers know how it felt to be alive, truly alive, he wondered.

Here in the northern half of the Canadian Province of Saskatchewan, which means quick flowing river in the Cree language, man remained insignificant and nature all powerful. Northern Saskatchewan is part of Canada's vast boreal forest, over a million square miles. An area over four times the size of Texas, and ten times bigger than the UK. A land stretching across the middle of the country, above the farms and prairies of southern Canada which border the USA, and below the treeless tundra further north. The territory contains innumerable lakes – thought to be a staggering one and a half million. The largest carbon dioxide storehouse on the planet, equivalent to nearly thirty years of man's emissions, and the largest intact forest on earth. In short, a place without equal.

Mingan, meaning gray wolf, was a Cree, the largest First Nation group in Canada. His face was round with almost Asian features and his hair jet-black which he grew long and kept tied back in a ponytail. Like a typical Cree, he was quick to smile and had a strong sense of humor.

Part of the Woods Cree who inhabited the northern part of this huge Province, he had spent a few years in Saskatoon in the south of the Province but missed home too much to settle there. Though when he'd returned to his community, the scourge of unemployment, alcoholism, and drugs really struck him after living in the city where such things were not so immediately visible. Two hundred years of repression first by the British and then the Canadian government and lasting until beyond the middle of last century, had taken a heavy toll on Canada's original inhabitants. Land allocated to them had been taken away at will, children had been forced to go to schools far from home, and their languages and customs banned. Only relatively recently had their culture come to be celebrated by the Canadian authorities.

Mingan had chosen to go live in the "bush" to escape the sad fate many of his people had succumbed to. He'd first spent several months with Cree in Quebec, learning the skills that he would need and which so many no longer possessed.

Beaching his canoe on the edge of the lake, he picked up his catch of fish, and walked the few yards to the cabin which he had hewn from the forest. His partner, Abbie, a redhead with blue eyes and freckles greeted him at the door. He'd met Abbie in Saskatoon and invited her up here five summers ago. She had never left.

"Looks like you had a successful trip, hon," she smiled.

"Yeah, the fish are really biting today."

Their cabin was a simple three-room affair.

An accomplished carpenter, Mingan had made their furniture from the surrounding forest. Outside, their two-year-old son squealed with laughter while he ran around chasing several husky puppies. Delightful companions for him to play with, they barked happily. They had the characteristic white face with black around the eyes and the top of their head, reaching down in a point between the eyes.

The adult huskies lay on the ground nearby. They were full from the caribou meat which Abbie had recently fed them. Summer, when temperatures could reach the high seventies and mosquitoes appeared in their millions, was their least favorite time of year. In winter they came into their own, pulling Mingan's sled the twenty miles to the nearest settlement if supplies were needed.

Mingan and Abbie cherished their life here. In the short warm summer, they could swim naked in the lake. They had complete freedom out here with no neighbors for miles. During winter, they would spend more time inside, but wrapped up against the cold they would let the huskies exercise, pulling them on sleds, or go snowshoeing in forests of white and across frozen lakes. They had this corner of the world to themselves and considered themselves truly privileged.

They lived mainly on fish, caribou meat, and berries. The forest provided them with wood for fuel and their cabin, canoe, and sleds. Nature gave them everything they needed.

Abbie missed some of the comforts of city life, and once a year would head back to Saskatoon to visit family. But she had no regrets about giving up her former life to be with Mingan. Here life was simple but invigorating. The worries which she'd carried around in her head in the city seemed so irrelevant now. With her mind free from the pressures of urban living, her senses were heightened in this elemental place. There were no distractions. There was time to observe and appreciate the world, be it the ever-changing sky or the wildlife. They had found their piece of paradise. There was little risk of it being ruined. After all, they had nothing anyone else wanted.

CHAPTER 6

Ann's motorcade drove through Ottawa. How British it all looked she thought, even the sky was gray with thick clouds. The Canadian Parliament seemed to be a French chateau version of the London one. Outside Rideau Hall, the official residence of the Canadian monarch and the Governor General, the King's representative in Canada, stood guards in the same red coats and tall black furry hats as those outside Buckingham Palace.

Ottawa, like Washington, was a compromise. Neither was a capital justified by economic importance. Washington had been chosen because it was a midway point between the original thirteen states along the eastern seaboard. Ottawa had been chosen as a place where English-speaking Canada met French-speaking Canada. Located in the backcountry away from the US border, it was thought easier to defend from possible American attack when it was named the capital in the 1850s.

Her car passed through the gates of 24

Sussex Drive, the Prime Minister's residence. Like some country house uprooted from Scotland or Wales, it was a large, light gray limestone building with a darker gray roof in four acres of wooded parkland on the south bank of the Ottawa River. Inside, Prime Minister Michael Beaumont got out of the swimming pool. He felt passively aggressive today. He had decided to be late deliberately. Who did she think she was, insisting that they meet immediately? Yet when one lived next to the world's biggest military power, which spent almost as much on defense as the rest of the world combined, and was told it was a matter of national security that couldn't wait, it was difficult to refuse. Michael didn't know what she wanted, but he was sure it would be something that wouldn't be to Canada's advantage.

Ann was shown to the library and offered coffee. The room, like the whole residence, conveyed an impression of faded glory. While she sat waiting, she ruminated on the relationship between these two giant size nations. Canada was an enigma to most Americans, a land which had chosen not to join them in the fight for independence. That they would have made that choice and still have kept the British monarch as head of state over two hundred and fifty years later was incomprehensible. Quaint maybe, but very odd. Yet many Americans, Ann included, had a sneaking admiration for what they had created, a country which seemed more at ease with itself than its always restless southern neighbor.

"Ann! How are you?"

Michael marched purposefully toward her, not bothering to apologize for being half an hour late. She stood up from her chair and he kissed her lightly on the cheek.

He was a ruddy-faced man with brown hair in his mid-forties. Like many of his fellow countrymen, he loved the great outdoors. In winter, incognito with a hat and scarf hiding his identity, he would join the crowds skating along the Rideau Canal, and in summer take his two teenage boys on camping trips to the country's endless supply of lakes.

"I'm good," she said as they both sat down. She was irritated at having been kept waiting for so long but expressing that would not help achieve her task. "Thank you for seeing me on short notice. How are the kids?"

"They're doing great. Look, Ann, I don't mean to be rude but I'm really very short of time. You've come alone?" He was perturbed to see there were no officials hovering around her as normal.

"Yes, I wanted to talk to you in private,

without aides. May I suggest you leave yours outside too?"

"Okay, if that's what you prefer."

"As you're in a hurry, let me get straight to the point. You'll already know California and the Southwest of my country face a water deficit. We've recently discovered we have a much more serious water shortage than previously thought. We need to act now or the region's economy could implode with a ripple effect around the world which would hurt Canada too. I'm here to ask for your help."

"Ann, you know our position on water exports. Canadians are very much opposed to them. I can't be seen to go against that."

"I understand, Michael, but we're your closest ally and biggest trading partner, and we need your co-operation. Let me at least show you our plan. The amount of water required would barely make a difference to you."

She took her device from her tote bag and displayed a map showing Canada and the US with a line running from northern Canada to the Colorado River.

"What's that line?" asked the Prime Minister, anticipating her reply but wanting to play dumb.

"It's a pipeline. We would like to build a

pipeline starting in the Northwest Territories running from Great Bear Lake to Great Slave Lake and on to Lake Athabasca in Northern Alberta and Saskatchewan, and then from there to the border. Right now the water just flows out into the Arctic Ocean."

"Why not take what you need from your own resources?"

"We've looked at that but it just doesn't add up. We'd have opposition-"

"Oh, I get it," said Michael. "You'd face opposition at home so you just thought you could take our water. Never mind the Canucks, they'll do what we tell them, eh?"

"I can appreciate how you must see it but to be frank we're screwed, and you're our only viable option. Why is your water so goddamn sacred, Michael? You're more than happy to sell us your oil and rip up the land to build gigantic open cast mines without regard to the environmental impact. You've got more water than you could ever want or need in places where no one lives and hardly ever goes. There's enough water in the Great Slave and Great Bear lakes to keep the Southwest going for over a hundred years. And we have plans for other sources: huge desalination plants, less wastage, water from Alaska and so on."

Ann was winging it but she also knew she excelled at that. She hadn't grown a multi-billion dollar company by being hesitant. She could see that she had Michael's attention, and from his expression it looked as if his hostility was softening so she upped the sales pitch.

"It would only be temporary until we get those other sources in place. Ten years max, maybe only five."

"Ann, even if I wanted to help you I couldn't. It would be political suicide, my own party would kick me to the curb faster than a puck in a hockey game. The government of Canada wouldn't even vote in favor of water as a human right at the UN. We didn't want to do anything that might open us up to you guys having a claim on our water resources."

"I totally understand. That's why the President wants it kept under wraps. You should only share this with those who you can really trust."

"And you think you could keep it under wraps?"

"For sure, that's mighty unpopulated country up there. We can put sections underground, and take it over ground reserved for the military."

"And the cold, have you thought about the

conditions up there? It makes a Chicago winter seem like the Caribbean."

"It will be a smart pipeline able to respond to climatic variations. Over fifty years ago, we put men on the moon. With today's technology, building it isn't going to be a problem if a decision is made to do it. Think what would happen if you refused. If California's agricultural sector collapsed, there'd be serious shortages of many foods and huge price rises. If people's properties down there became worthless overnight imagine the repercussions. The global economy is already on the brink. We're your most important market. If we take a big hit, you'll be down and out too."

She could tell from his demeanor that Michael understood so she decided to close.

"I need an answer, Michael, we don't have the luxury of time. I'd like to come back in a few days for your decision. If you have any questions, day or night, you have my private number. Please understand, it's a matter of utmost importance to the United States. Our national security is at stake."

"Your national security? So what you really mean is if I don't agree, you'll come and take it by force anyway."

"Those are your words, not mine. This is not

a zero sum game. We'd pay market price for the water. You would have billions of dollars coming in. Not only that, the President has authorized me to say that if you help us, we'll help you in return. He's willing to speak out against Quebec's independence referendum this fall, say that we consider it bad for the continent and that he wouldn't allow them into our free trade deal. That would be economic disaster for them. You know the vote's going to be close, and what he says could make all the difference."

"And the Arctic Ocean?"

Ann continued to improvise. She hadn't cleared what she was saying with the President but if he wanted her to make a deal, he would have to accept concessions.

"I'm sure that he'll be willing to be generous with your claims to territorial waters in the Arctic. So, can I return in a few days time for an answer?"

"Resources are matters for the Provinces, not the federal government."

"I'm sure you can figure that out. We can't let a few people stand in the way of something this important to both our countries."

Ann put away her device and stood up.

"Thank you for your time, Prime Minister. I

do hope I can count on you."

She gave a perfunctory smile and departed. Michael remained seated, feeling as if a tornado had just passed right through him. What was he to do?

Canada and the USA were allies by location, not necessarily by choice. Until united in the common cause of World War Two and afterward by the Cold War against Russia, they had been potential adversaries.

Before then America's biggest rival had been Britain and its empire, the closest part of which was Canada. War Plan Red, developed in the late 1920s, planned for what would happen if there was a war between the USA and the British Empire, known as the Reds. An invasion would start with a poisonous gas attack on Halifax in Nova Scotia, to deny British troops access to Canada. Other fronts would involve attacks on Toronto to destroy the country's industrial base and on the railways in Winnipeg.

Not to be outdone, the Canadians already had their own plan, Defense Scheme No.1, to launch attacks on Seattle, Minneapolis, and Albany if an invasion seemed likely. They knew that they couldn't hold them but hoped to divert American resources until re-enforcements from Britain arrived. While retreating, they would destroy bridges to delay the American advance.

Canada's approach was amateur by comparison with an annual budget of only one thousand dollars for their protagonist, who collected free maps in gas stations south of the border for use in the event of war. In 1931, Canada abandoned its plan, recognizing that any struggle with the US would not be winnable.

There remained speculation about whether America still had a plan to attack Canada if ever needed. The Prime Minister didn't know the answer, but he was certain if there wasn't one already in place that they would be working on it in the Pentagon.

As long ago as the 1950s, a retired Canadian general had remarked that eventually the USA was going to need Canada's water so they should figure out how to sell it to them before they invaded and took it anyway. But water is the very essence of Canada, deeply ingrained in its identity. From the glacier-fed turquoise lakes in the Rockies to the raging rapids of countless rivers across the country, from spectacular waterfalls to the frozen water of the North where the polar bear roams. Now the Prime Minister was being asked to compromise one of the defining characteristics of his nation. Once that particular dam was breached, even if only a little, exactly how much would their American cousins want until they were satisfied? At first some for the Southwest, just to tide them over so they said, then some for Texas, then some to water the crops on the vast farms of the Great Plains. Where would it all end?

Michael walked out of the house and down to the banks of the Ottawa River. Whenever he faced a difficult problem, he found that watching the water flow past helped his thought processes. He knew there would be a furor if he agreed to their demands. When it became public knowledge, he would be finished. America could go to hell. It was their problem, not Canada's. A surge of anger ran through him at Ann's audacity for suggesting his country should bail them out for the mess they had got themselves into. They had wrongly assumed that they could come crying to Canada like a spoiled child, demanding water.

Yet he loved his country and he also understood that saying no wasn't a realistic option. America wasn't going to sit idly by while California and the Southwest returned to empty desert and its economy collapsed. If he said no, they would come and get what they wanted, and he didn't see the point of wasting the blood of one Canadian over it. Like Ann had said, Canada had more water than it could possibly want. After all, it wouldn't make much difference to let them have a little for a few years.

No, that wasn't right, giving into a bully...

his mind twirled with the arguments in favor and against. He decided to sleep on it. Things would be clearer come morning.

CHAPTER 7

Angel was on a high. He had a whole week off from his monotonous job flipping burgers. He was driving north to South Dakota to a powwow. He wouldn't know anyone, but he had always wanted to go there and with his ancestry he felt confident of a warm welcome.

After a couple of very long days on the road through the awesome open spaces of Utah, Colorado, and Nebraska, and a night sleeping under the stars in his pickup, he had reached South Dakota, home of the Oglala Lakota Sioux. He experienced a thrill when he got his first glimpse of the campground on the horizon. Many tipis had been erected. When he got closer, he could see several Native Americans walking around in their traditional clothes and great headdresses of feathers.

The land was open and dry. As dry as Arizona it seemed, although covered in grass which was now colored a light brown from the heat of summer. The sky towered above, indescribably large. Gigantic white clouds drifted by, changing shape while the wind pushed them from west to east.

But beyond the tipis and colorful traditional clothing, the landscape collided with reality, the poverty of the reservation: rusting trailers, abandoned cars, and piles of junk.

Finding a place to park – he had no tent and would sleep in the truck – he got out to explore. Angel walked around in something of a daze, lost to the world by the sights all around him and fatigue from his long trip.

"Wematin!"

A woman's desperate cry of anguish abruptly snapped him out of his trance.

Out of the corner of his eye, he saw a small boy no more than two years old running into the path of an oncoming vehicle oblivious to the danger. The driver clearly hadn't seen the child about to cross his path either. As quick as an eagle swooping on its prey, Angel leaped toward the boy, grabbing him with his arms and fell back onto the earth holding the boy above him just as the truck passed by. Gently, he put him back on the ground. The little boy kicked and screamed in frustration that his bid for freedom had been thwarted.

His mother arrived and her child went gratefully into the safety of her arms as she bent down to pick him up. From his vantage point, he looked at the stranger who had rescued him with undisguised resentment.

"Wematin, you mustn't run off. That truck would have hit you if this man here hadn't stopped you."

The boy, now feeling embarrassed, began crying and buried his face in his mother's chest. A man joined them.

"Thank you so much," he said to Angel who was now standing and dusting himself down. "You saved our little boy's life."

"Anyone would have done the same."

"Maybe but you're the one who did. I'm Mingan," he said offering his hand. "This here's my partner, Abbie, and Wematin, our son."

"Hi, I'm Angel."

"We'd be honored if you could join us to eat later. It's the least we can do to thank you."

"Sure, that would be great."

"Come on over in about an hour. Our tent is that one over there."

Early that evening, they sat on the ground outside the tent eating burgers from Mingan's barbecue.

"What brings you here?" asked Mingan.

"I live in Phoenix. My father was Apache. I wanted to come up here and experience Native American culture. And you?"

"I'm a Cree. We're from Northern Saskatchewan. We've been in Saskatoon visiting Abbie's parents and thought it would be cool to come here to the powwow so we borrowed their van and camping gear."

"What do you make of it?"

"To be honest, it makes me sad to see how our brothers are living down here just like it makes me sad to see how so many of my own people live. That's why we chose to move into the forest, away from the reservation. If we try to live like the white man it doesn't work. Their way of life wasn't our way – we end up drunk and on handouts. I believe our salvation lies in living the same way our ancestors did, not to try and live like others. Our way of life worked for thousands of years, we need to get back to it and stop living the life of victims and blaming others."

"You do have a point," agreed Angel. "But maybe in Canada you have the space to do that. In America, most land is privately owned, and our reservations are in the worst places. Living like our forefathers is not really an option."

He was right of course, the original inhabitants of this country had been left with what everyone else didn't want. Here on the Pine Ridge reservation, part of which is on the Badlands – the clue's in the name - there is little land suitable for agriculture. It was what remained of a much larger territory given to the Oglala Sioux following their defeat. The reservation had been drastically reduced in size over the years when westward moving settlers demanded ever more land for themselves. As Chief Red Cloud noted: "The white man made us many promises, more than I can remember, but they never kept but one: they promised to take our land, and they took it."

Like the San Carlos reservation in Arizona, home of Angel's deceased father, Pine Ridge reservation was one of the poorest places in the country with an average life expectancy of around fifty. Over the years there had been sporadic outbreaks of violence between residents and law enforcement authorities. The place was a tinderbox of tension.

Much of the poverty could be traced back to the Bureau of Indian Affairs. Native American nations were supposedly nations within the USA but they weren't not left to run their own country. Their lands were managed by the federal government and a system created in the nineteenth century when the white man had completed his conquests, born of the notion that Native Americans couldn't be trusted to handle their own affairs.

Much of the land was fractionated. Federal law required land be passed in equal shares to multiple heirs. After a few generations, land ownership had become impossible to establish. Often hundreds would have an interest in each piece of land so it languished undeveloped and unproductive. Unable to prove title, those living there couldn't use the land as collateral to raise loans to build homes or provide money to start a business. Alcoholism, mass unemployment, and drug abuse were the self-perpetuating symptoms of vested interests.

"Well, that's enough preaching from me for one evening. Let's enjoy the energy here tonight," said Mingan. "We'll just clean up and then go on down to watch the dancing."

They sat mesmerized, watching tens of dancers chanting and gyrating to drums, silhouetted by the night and the light cast by the burning fires. It was easy to imagine they had been transported back in time two hundred years to when the plains echoed to the thunder of stampeding buffalo herds, estimated to be a staggering fifty million at the start of the nineteenth century. A time before the settlers left their homes on the Eastern seaboard seeking a new life on the frontier and changing the lives of the original inhabitants forever.

Observing the dancing, Angel thought of nearby Wounded Knee. In 1890, a movement took hold amongst Native Americans known as ghost dancing. They believed that dancing day and night would make them invincible to the army's bullets, and bring back the dead warriors and also the buffalo driven to the verge of extinction by the white man to starve Native Americans into submission. Fearing ghost dancing would encourage rebellion amongst the tribes, only recently corralled onto reservations to keep them under control and dependent on government handouts, the authorities ordered it be stamped out. And at Wounded Knee, it was. Some three hundred and fifty men, women, and children were massacred while they tried to flee the army's bullets. The snow was stained red with their blood. It was only four days after Christmas, and marked a painful end to the centuries of conflict which began when the first Europeans had arrived in North America to claim the continent as their own, ignoring the fact that it already belonged to others.

Angel felt a strong empathy for these people. Not just those who lived here, but all Native Americans who fell and stumbled in today's world. For them, the American dream was often more a nightmare.

He thought of how he'd been beaten up and called names, and was still mocked and assaulted for embracing his heritage. An antipathy toward the modern world had grown in him, one that had increased as he'd learned how the West was won by killing and subjugating the Native American.

Angel didn't know how he could change things, but that night he promised himself he would find a way to make a difference. Helping those whose blood ran through his veins was what made him feel a passion and a sense of what he wanted to do with his life. The positivity of American culture had instilled in him a belief that anything was possible, that you didn't have to accept things as they were. They could be whatever you wanted them to be so long as you were prepared to do whatever it took to make it happen.

They sat watching the dancing late into the night.

"Hey, Angel we're gonna hit the sack," said Mingan. "We're driving back to Canada first thing tomorrow."

"It's been a real pleasure to spend time with you all."

"Abbie and I have been talking. We'd really love for you to come visit, show you how we live. We don't bother with cell or wifi up there even though they tell us with all those satellites they now have, we could get connected. Take this, I've written down the name of the settlement nearest us. You need to take a float plane from Saskatoon. There are no roads where we live. Come in summer and you can get a ride out to our place by canoe, or if you come in winter, you can get there by dog sled or snowmobile."

"That sounds awesome. I'd totally love to do that."

"Well, make sure you come and soon."

"You bet. Have a safe trip home."

Angel watched them go, hoping he would see them again. He lingered for a little longer, still enjoying the mystical atmosphere of this special night.

CHAPTER 8

The President was meeting with Chip and Kim Chan, his National Security Adviser. He was seated at his desk, the Resolute desk, named after the British frigate HMS Resolute. After being frozen in Arctic ice and abandoned, the ship had been recovered by American sailors. Refurbished, it was presented as a gift from the United States to Queen Victoria. When the British navy decommissioned the Resolute, she ordered twin desks be made from it. Keeping one for herself, she gave the other to the then President, Rutherford Hayes. However, had she been alive today, she would most certainly not have been amused by what was being discussed around that very piece of furniture.

"Ann tells me she thinks the Prime Minister will agree to my request with the right concessions. It seems they want me to speak out against Quebec's independence. I don't really have a problem with that. Having to deal with another country of irascible French people isn't my idea of fun, nor do I have a huge problem agreeing their claims to territorial waters in the Arctic which they have also asked for."

"That wouldn't be so great," interjected Kim, who at thirty-two was an extremely young holder of her post.

"Maybe not, but I would insist on a national security exception. Anyway, I need us to be fully prepared for all eventualities so tell me what you've got."

"Well, if we run into trouble and political pressure fails, we believe our aim should be to keep any conflict as low-key as possible," said Chip.

"I agree totally, conflict with Canada would shake everyone's faith in our trustworthiness," added Kim.

"Our plan would be to enforce a fifty-mile exclusion zone either side of the planned route for the pipeline. We would send a significant force in to leave them in no doubt that we have the means to prevail but the strong desire to avoid any fighting," said Chip.

"Mr. President, it's not for me to tell you how to do your job but have you thought this through?" asked Kim. "Under the War Powers Resolution, you can't commit military forces for more than sixty days without the approval of Congress."

"I know, Kim. I'll deal with that if it happens. If it all goes wrong and we come to blows, I think the American people will understand why I had to keep it confidential, why broadcasting what we are doing would have been so damaging. If I made this public, I'd kill investment in California and the Southwest and cause a property crash within twenty-four hours. Do you think folks would thank me for that? Sure they'd feel uncomfortable that we were in conflict with our friend up North, but I believe they would think protecting California and the Southwest from collapse takes precedence. I'm confident they would agree I'd done the right thing by getting on and dealing with the problem."

"But we're not talking about some Iraq or Afghanistan here. People can identify with Canadians, they're like us."

"I get that but folks will understand that the Canadians have more water than they could possibly ever need and they could help us, and if they won't then we have to help ourselves. We can't let the future of the United States depend on preserving a wilderness that's bigger than anyone can possibly explore even if they spent a whole lifetime doing it."

Kim remained unhappy.

"What about the rest of the world? The Europeans would go apeshit, and of more concern the Chinese would take it as a sign that they were fully justified in going in and taking what they wanted in their own neighborhood."

Jackson was fast becoming irritated, it was time to remind her who was boss. He stood up to assert his authority.

"I appreciate your concern Kim, but I expect you to fully support my decision. What's the latest on the pipeline build, Chip?"

"We reckon if we get the green light next week, we can have units in place within forty-eight hours preparing the ground. Wherever possible we'd cut through forest, out of sight, and underground in areas closer to towns. We'll be using the military to do the build to reduce risk of discovery. We've already placed initial orders for pipes. The first deliveries should be coming through within a month. There's plenty of government land on both sides of the border which we can use."

"Sounds good. How long until it's operational?"

"Initially, our plan is only to build it to feed the upper reaches of the Colorado and use the river to do the rest of the job. Given that winter will slow down construction, our best guess is eighteen to twenty-four months."

"That's cutting it close if the data we have is

correct. I need you to throw whatever resources are needed at it. I don't want to take all this risk and still face watergeddon. That really would piss off the voters."

"I understand. We won't let you down."

"Right, I need to jet. Alexandra and I have a love-in with the British Prime Minister starting in ten minutes."

"The Brits, now that'll create some fireworks. The King of England is the King of Canada too. We'd be invading his country," said Kim unable to stop herself.

"Well, they can huff and puff all they like but it won't make any difference. The Brits are pragmatic. They'll be more upset with the Canadians for being so difficult. You know, Kim, I want to hear solutions, not problems. If you want to remain part of this administration, you'll need to become a more positive person."

CHAPTER 9

Maria Fuentes drove up the to the hotel entrance. She handed the keys to the valet and strolled to check in.

"My partner will be here later this evening," she explained to the receptionist.

"No problem. You have our best room. I think you'll love it. It is gorgeous, believe me. Okay, you're all set. Toby will take you up."

The receptionist was right. The room was a delight, floor to ceiling windows looking toward the mountains and a hot tub on the balcony. The bathroom was bigger than her living room at home; a massive walk-in shower and a large tub for two.

Maria didn't pay much attention while Toby went onto autopilot with his over-rehearsed explanation of the amenities. After he left, she kicked off her shoes and jumped backward onto the king size bed. It felt like floating on a cloud, it was so comfortable. She was on a weekend in a luxury hotel in Palm Springs with her boss.

He wasn't the perfect long term partner but who was. Too often in her past she'd fallen for losers. although she thought he was cheap for choosing Palm Springs in summer. It would be way too hot to lie out by the pool during the day.

It would be a few hours until he got here so she undressed, put on one of the white robes from the closet, and made her way to the spa for some pampering to get her in the right mood. As she lay there relishing her treatments, she reminisced about her life.

Maria had started life in the slums of a small town in northern Mexico. Following the death of her parents in a fire when she was only a teenager, she and her brother, Emilio, headed to the US for the chance of a better life. Three times they crossed the border in populated areas, and three times they were caught and sent back. Repeated failure made them realize they needed help so they gave all the money which they had to a guy who promised to get them across.

He got them over at night, somewhere in the empty desert of southern Arizona where the border wasn't regularly patrolled. They had made it but they were in the middle of nowhere. He abandoned them, saying he'd done what he had said he would do and left them without any water.

When dawn came, they began walking. They

followed dusty, dried-up arroyos pushing their way through mesquites whose thorns tore at their flesh. Their tongues were swollen in their dry mouths. The sun targeted them like a laser with intense heat from sunup until sundown, and a hot wind raised the temperature even higher, increasing their all consuming thirst.

Later in the day, their hopes rose as the sky darkened and the thunder rolled. A spectacular electric storm played out far above them. But nature was only tormenting them. No rain fell, it had evaporated in the hot air above them long before it could reach the ground. Though they walked and walked they could find no sign of life, and no water. They walked until they could go no farther, exhausted and dehydrated. They lay down that night, bereft of hope and closed their eyes fully expecting to die.

Morning came and they were still alive, just. The day offered no respite, the sun as fierce as ever. They got up to walk again but stumbled and fell so often they gave up and lay down to surrender to their fate. Both of them blacked out.

Maria awoke to a soothing voice speaking Spanish and telling her to drink. Her throat was so dry it hurt to swallow. She wondered if she had died and was in heaven, but as her eyes focused she saw she was still in hell right here on earth. The good Samaritan had come too late for

Emilio.

The man took her to his ranch house outside Tucson. He too had come from Mexico many years ago. Although distraught about the loss of her brother, Maria was grateful to have survived and to the man who had saved her. Elderly, he lived alone, his wife having died some years ago. Maria stayed with him, cleaning his house and cooking his meals. A kind man, he treated her as if she was his daughter, and he taught her English. Then one day she found him dead in his bed.

His son, who had never bothered to visit him when he was alive, soon arrived from LA and demanded she leave immediately. She gathered her few possessions and left taking the bus to Phoenix. When she first arrived, she lived on the streets, hungry and alone. Eventually, she found work and could afford to rent a room that she shared with three other undocumented immigrants.

Maria wiped a tear from her face while she remembered. Over the years she had made a life for herself. A short marriage to an American citizen had given her the right to stay. Now she had a decent home in the suburbs, an automobile, and a boss who showered her with life's luxuries and was going to leave his wife for her. She had a wealthier life than she could ever have hoped for in Mexico. But a happier one, well she wasn't so sure of that. Maria had no real friends and had found no real sense of community where she lived. People were all so busy pursuing the dream, working such long hours. Most had plenty of money and material things but little time just to be.

When Maria returned to the room, she ordered champagne from room service and had them place it out by the hot tub. Night was falling and it would soon be cool enough to be outside. She slipped into a black silk negligee. She looked in the mirror and smiled. For a woman in her mid-forties, she was still hot. Her jet black hair, now colored every few weeks at the salon, cascaded on to her shoulders. Her face was still round and youthful and her body was in good shape, even if helped by botox and her breast implants. Maria felt gorgeous and sexy. The door opened and he entered.

"My, ain't you a sight for sore eyes," he grinned.

"Do you think so?" she asked playfully as she slipped out of her negligee, throwing it on the floor and turning deliberately slowly away from him. "Why don't you join me in the jacuzzi for champagne?"

He watched in delight as she walked naked toward the balcony. Quickly ripping his clothes off, he joined her in the bubbles. They soon forgot about the champagne.

Later that night in bed, she looked across at him. The moon outside cast a pale light into their room. He was certainly no Hollywood movie star to look at, and though he might be the Governor of Arizona, he snored worse than any man she had ever slept with.

CHAPTER 10

Prime Minister Beaumont usually met with his ministers in the Langevin block or his offices in Parliament, however the topic for discussion was so secret that he had called those he felt he could really trust to his home. Paul Charlier, Minister of National Defense and Erik Falsdag, his Minister of Finance were there. He'd wanted to invite Hannah Blake, his Minister of Foreign Affairs, but he had doubts that she could be trusted to keep their discussions confidential.

"As you may have heard, I had a visit the other day from the US Secretary of State. I have asked you here because this is a matter of critical importance to our country, one that could so easily end badly if it isn't handled correctly. It also needs to be kept totally secret, not for any ulterior motive but to avoid it all going wrong and having disastrous consequences."

He explained what the giant on their border required of them.

"Can't say I'm surprised," said Erik. "It was

only a question of when, not if. We've all known this day would come. What have you decided?"

The Prime Minister advised them of his decision.

"I'll support you, Michael."

"Me too," said Paul.

Later that afternoon, Ann arrived back in Ottawa. Michael's welcome was formal this time, no kiss on the cheek or exchange of pleasantries. As she sat down in the armchair opposite him, a sudden rush of doubt ran through her. Was he going to say no? She hoped fervently that he wouldn't. A refusal could lead to a conflict she had never envisaged as possible. One that would shake the foundations of all that had been assumed by Americans and Canadians while they'd lived in peace side by side for so many years. War was something that didn't happen in North America. It was something which had plagued Europe last century, and still plagued countries on the periphery of world politics today, but not those at its center of gravity.

"I shall say yes, but with conditions. We will allow you to take water of an amount we agree upon for ten years maximum while you develop alternative sources. In return, I'll accept your offer of help in undermining support for the Parti Quebecois in the independence referendum in November, and I need you to agree our territorial claims in the Arctic. I also have a couple more requests in mind too, trade disputes I want your government to drop."

Michael would gamble that when the news broke as surely it must, he could demonstrate to the country the government had secured the best deal possible, and that the alternative would have been far worse. He believed saying no would lead to economic hardship, very possibly war, and maybe even the end of Canada. He would need to involve the Premier of Saskatchewan. Fortunately he was a good and trusted friend. As for the Northwest Territories, that would be more difficult but he was confident it could be done.

Ann dropped her shoulders in relief. There would be no conflict after all.

"Thank you, Prime Minister. I'm sure the President will look favorably on your proposals. We will be in touch very soon about the logistics of getting the pipeline started. This is a good day for both our countries."

"No, this is not a good day, Secretary of State. Your government is blackmailing us, holding a gun to our head. The consequences of all this may soon be out of our control, and lead us all to regret what today we have started. Would you please leave now."

Ann left feeling deflated. Yes, the President would be delighted with her but at what cost for everyone? Having updated him by phone on the flight back to Washington, she was driven to her home in Georgetown, an elegant nineteenth-century red brick house with black wooden shutters either side of the windows and a white portico above the front door.

An anxiety which refused to go away gnawed at her. Ann had always believed in what she had been tasked to achieve. Even though she'd secured all that she had been required to, she was uncomfortable. She had succeeded but Ann felt no satisfaction. She needed to relax, enjoy a rare moment of tranquility in her demanding life.

Her house had been furnished by a top designer, each room a statement of classic elegance, however since the last of her three children had moved out it was too quiet. No longer a family home, it had become an extension of her office. Ann and her husband had divorced a year ago, and while that had been of her choosing, she missed coming home to someone. A famous person on the world stage, an icon to many, she personified to many women how to have it all. But when she came home she was a nobody, just another of the millions of middle-aged people across the country living by themselves, lonely and left wondering as they looked back to happier times past, was that it?

Had all their dreams and ambition come to this, cast adrift in a sea of solitude?

Ann poured herself a glass of wine and ran a bath. Both of these usually lifted her spirits but the drink and warm water didn't do it for her this time. She needed company, a human touch.

Ann dressed and drove across town. She parked and hurried across the street head down, not wanting to be recognized, and went up the steps to the front door of a row house. Opening it with the key he'd given her, Ann climbed the stairs to the second floor and knocked on the door to an apartment. A tall, young man with chiseled features and two days of stubble opened it.

"Hi, Ethan. I hope you don't mind me showing up unannounced?"

"No, not at all. Come on in. Can I get you a drink?"

"Later perhaps," she said grabbing his belt and pulling him toward her so she could kiss him. She began tugging at his clothing. He responded in kind and led her to his bed, which he hadn't made since yesterday.

As Ethan lay down on top of her, Ann felt herself melt under the weight of him, able to forget if only for a few minutes all that tormented her inner being while she abandoned herself in the moment and clung tightly to him.

She'd met Ethan when he had worked as an intern in the Department of State last summer. One evening, he stayed late to help Ann finish an important briefing paper for the Commander in Chief in the Harry S. Truman Building in DC's Foggy Bottom district. Ann drove him to his home, accepted his invitation for a drink which had turned into several, and they'd spent their first night together.

She knew he dated women his own age and that she was just a fling to him. Ann would never find real love with Ethan, but she couldn't control herself as far as he was concerned.

He was her escape from a reality she no longer wanted to acknowledge. A method of coping, her drug, her addiction. A way of clinging to her youth, which in retrospect had passed her by in fast motion without her even noticing, and was now only a memory somewhere beyond the horizon behind her.

CHAPTER 11

Paige Delamere was a lover of the great outdoors. She'd stationed herself for the summer on the edge of Yellowknife in the Northwest Territories, driving a thousand miles from Alberta to get there, and yielding to the buffalo that nonchalantly crossed the empty highway. The only town of any size in the whole of the NWT, Yellowknife sat on the northern edge of Great Slave Lake. It was so vast a region, the tiny capital was but a dot in this huge land. As the tourist authority proudly proclaimed, NWT put the "W" in wilderness, and for once this was no exaggeration. This untamed country stretched into the tundra and the shores of the Arctic Ocean. A land where the sun stayed below the horizon in mid winter, and never left the sky in mid summer. A land whose enormity and emptiness defied human comprehension.

Paige might be living in an RV these days but she was no crunchy-hippie. She was a woman who loved to look good even in the boonies. Paige had perfected the art of how to look fabulous when in the wild. Maybe it was that fresh water which she bathed in, preferring a lake to a camp shower anytime. It made her complexion smoother than any expensive face cream ever could, and her long auburn hair shine and hang in natural waves down beyond her shoulders as if she'd spent hundreds of dollars in a top end salon.

Originally from Boston, she coasted through Yale and spent five years working at the US embassies in Beijing and Cairo. In both postings she'd witnessed the problems caused by insufficient water resources. In China, she saw the dust bowl sweeping south and eastward across the country and growing ever bigger as man exploited the land in a reckless way, disrupting the delicate balance of the natural world which had once kept the desert at bay. In Egypt, she saw a country only habitable along a narrow band either side of the Nile with an ever growing population, which strained even the ability of that great river to support it while the country lurched from crisis to crisis, becoming ever poorer and more radicalized.

Since her return to the US a year ago, she'd become an active blogger, an advocate of environmental causes. Paige wanted to connect with people who shared the views which she expressed. Water, or rather the lack of it, was her new focus. Her latest blogs warned of the risk of

Canada's water being sold to the United States. How would her readers feel about that? Would they be prepared to do anything to stop it? Many had responded. Americans didn't see why it should be a problem. Canadians were very much against it. But few of them seemed to have the motivation to do something to stop it, and even fewer were willing to talk with her in person about it.

Paige was demoralized by the apathy she was getting, so arriving back at her RV one late summer evening she was pleased to have a new message from a guy who sounded really passionate about the issue. He viewed the idea as another example of seizing resources which belonged to North America's original inhabitants, something he vehemently opposed. She messaged him back and they soon became firm virtual friends. He went by the name of Angel Tarak. Although he lived in Phoenix, he intended to visit Saskatchewan next year and they made tentative plans to meet up.

CHAPTER 12

The President had never spoken at a meeting of the Canadian Bar Association. The organizers of its annual convention were thrilled, even if rather surprised, to receive news only yesterday that he, rather than the US ambassador to Canada, would be addressing the delegates. Brian Altman, the President of the CBA, had received a full briefing, and the major networks had been notified by the White House press office to be there. No explanation was given but they knew better than to ignore such a tip off.

Brian wondered why the man was coming. Sure, there were several thousand Canadian lawyers here in Nashville which was good for its tourism industry, but that was hardly worthy of the attention of the President of the United States.

The following morning, the first indication the President had arrived was the presence of numerous secret service men. A few moments later, Jackson breezed in from a side door and bounded up the stairs onto the podium, shaking hands with Brian and others seated on the stage. The audience broke into spontaneous applause, everyone straining to get a view of someone who they felt like they knew already yet wanting to see what he actually looked like in the flesh.

Brian welcomed their esteemed guest.

"Thank you, Chairman Aldridge," the President began, quite unaware that he had got both his name and title wrong. "And I'd like to say thank you to each and every one of you here today for giving me the opportunity to address this hallowed organization representing the Canadian legal profession. It is, after all, the rule of law and the great work that each of you does which upholds the great democratic traditions and freedoms which we hold so dear here in North America. Two countries with shared values. Our friendship and co-operation showing a fractured world what our planet could be like if others followed our example."

His platitudes continued for quite some time, and when it seemed that was all he was going to offer, his speech took an unexpected turn.

"The United States benefits from a strong and united Canada. I believe it's no exaggeration to say that our national security depends on it. It is therefore of very serious concern to the government of the United States that there is a risk that your great country could be thrown into turmoil and division should the people of Quebec vote for independence in the referendum taking place in a few weeks time.

"I wanted to come here today to make it clear that I don't consider it would be in anyone's interests, including those of the people of Quebec, were they to vote to leave Canada. My government would not support such a move, and would not accept an independent Quebec into the United States - Mexico - Canada free trade agreement. Moreover, the right of those in Quebec who didn't want to be subsumed into some new state against their will would have to be recognized. I refer not only to the First Nations in Quebec, who have made plain their opposition to being forced out of Canada, but also those in the western part of the Province whose affinity is firmly with the rest of Canada. The American government takes the view that if Quebec can secede from Canada, there is no reason that those areas of Quebec opposed to secession could not also secede from Quebec, and choose to remain Canadian."

The sense of shock amongst the delegates was almost audible. The US had always taken the view that this was an internal matter for Canada. Such a complete reversal of policy and in such a public and uncompromising fashion was completely unexpected.

"I therefore hope and pray that the good people of Quebec will vote to stay within Canada and recognize that together we are stronger. God bless Canada!"

Shaking hands again with Brian Altman, Ted Jackson left to the sound of muffled applause. The networks swung into action immediately, leaving Brian lost for words as they fought to interview him about a subject he wanted to avoid expressing any opinion on.

In Quebec, the leader of the Parti Quebecois was almost speechless too but with incandescent rage, denouncing foreign interference and economic blackmail. The vote was likely to have been close. This intervention would surely tip the balance toward a 'no' majority. People tended to vote with their pocket. The US stance would seriously damage the economy of Quebec if they voted for independence.

Prime Minister Beaumont, on the other hand, was pleased and congratulated himself that his gamble was beginning to pay off. In DC, Republican party strategists were confused.

"Exactly what game is the President playing?" asked Buzz Guthrie, the septuagenarian Chairman of the Republican National Committee.

"I'd sure as hell would like to know,"

responded Dean Carson, the favorite to secure the Republican nomination in next year's Presidential election. "Can I count on you and your boys to find out?"

"Sure Dean, I'll do a little digging."

Buzz would do all that he could to help him. They were fellow Texans, both from the conservative wing of the party. Buzz was Dean's father figure, and Dean the son who Buzz had never had. He also knew that if he helped Dean to win, he could have his pick of the top jobs in a new administration.

Dean left and Buzz stayed in his office, thinking. Why would the President make a stand on this? America was officially neutral on the issue, but if the truth be known the power bases in both parties weren't at all disturbed by the prospect of an independent Quebec. They knew it would have to fit in with the United States, which would be the dominant partner in the relationship, and Canada would surely be more malleable and less irritatingly smug if it lost Quebec. There must be some other influence at play here. What bargain had he struck with the Canadian government, and for what reason?

Buzz picked up the phone to a contact in the Department of State. Later that evening, in the comfort of his palatial home in Alexandria across the Potomac from the capital, he got a call.

“It seems the Secretary of State’s been up to Ottawa a few times recently, but there’s been no announcement about the visits by either side. They say on each occasion she met the Canadian Prime Minister at his private residence, alone.”

“Okay, good job. I’ll take it from here.”

Buzz made another call.

“Hi, it’s Buzz here. I need you to keep a close eye on the Secretary of State, you know the routine. Specifically, I need to know why she’s been undertaking unannounced visits to Canada. If you saw the news today, you’ll know the President’s done a one eighty on independence for Quebec and I want to know why.”

“Sure thing, but it’ll cost you.”

“The cost doesn’t matter so long as you get results. I’ll be waiting to hear, and soon.”

Buzz put the phone down and lit a cigar. He was determined to get to the bottom of this. There was something going down, something that they might just be able to use to their great advantage in next year’s Presidential campaign.

CHAPTER 13

By fall, American military engineers were already in location across Saskatchewan and several States in the western half of the USA. Under cover of darkness, huge digging machines and trucks loaded with pipes moved along highways. By morning all trace of them had vanished, leaving only vague memories amongst those living along their route of a deep rumble and flashing lights while they stirred in their sleep.

This would be one of the most challenging engineering projects of all time. Building a pipeline in the terrain it had to cross would not be easy. The approach of winter, already firmly in control along the northern half of the route, added to the difficulty.

For the last few months, a team directed from the Pentagon had been planning every aspect of 'Operation Bring It On Home'. Advance parties had already gone in weeks earlier to survey the planned route and make adjustments where necessary.

In a corner of remote Lake Athabasca, a camouflaged pumping station was under construction. From there, the pipelines would go through the backwoods of Saskatchewan to the US border and join a pipelines coming up from Colorado. The pipelines would be constructed using the latest reflective technology, making it almost impossible to see unless someone got close to it. Military units had cordoned off areas where risk of discovery was thought likely, and construction manpower had been supplemented by the latest available robots.

Prime Minister Beaumont had negotiated a good price for the water, and with that bought the co-operation of the Provincial governments in Yellowknife and Regina. Their economies were in recession and they needed extra revenues. Avoiding unpopular spending cuts and tax increases could keep the incumbents in power at the next election so persuasion hadn't been difficult.

The President received weekly reports on progress. It was early days but so far all was going according to plan.

In California and the Southwest, the longest drought in their recorded history continued and the water levels in the dams fell ever lower like water draining out of a bathtub. All were hoping for heavy snowfall and rain this winter to replenish them and ward off disaster.

Thousands of miles from both the freezing wastes of Northern Canada and the parched landscape of the Southwest, Ann reluctantly climbed out of the warm sanctuary of Ethan's bed. It was only five, but she needed to return home to get ready for an appearance at a UN conference in New York later that morning.

Why she'd confided in Ethan she didn't know. Was it because of the two bottles of wine they'd consumed the previous evening, or that she found the burden of office too great and needed to let off steam with someone she trusted?

Ethan dozed while she dressed. Ann had a splitting headache but she knew she had no choice but to ignore her hangover and get through the day. Gently, Ann touched Ethan's face to wake him.

"Hey, I have to go now. I just wanted to say all that stuff I told you, you do understand it's beyond confidential."

"Absolutely," he yawned and rolled over.

Ann shut the door quietly and went down the stairs. Opening the front door, she glanced furtively up and down the street. Night still immobilized the world. There was no one out walking, no traffic, only silence. As she hurried down the steps from the front door to the sidewalk and her parked car, she didn't notice the man in the black sedan across the street taking photos.

When she got back to her house, she glanced at herself in the bathroom mirror and grimaced. After her night of passion, she looked anything but America's popular and immaculately coiffured Secretary of State.

As rain filtered a gray dawn, she wanted nothing more than to go back to bed and be cocooned by her soft goose down pillows but that wasn't an option. She made the finishing touches to her makeup and rushed downstairs to meet her driver.

Across town, the same man who had photographed her, took several pictures of Ethan while he walked down the street to grab a coffee on his way to work. When Ethan emerged, the man got out of his car and followed him to his office.

CHAPTER 14

The weeks passed by. Out of sight, work on the pipelines progressed. Thanksgiving and the Holiday season came and went, and now it was already February. Politicians were going into overdrive. This was, after all, the year of a Presidential election.

In Phoenix, Maria was a woman scorned. As she sat at her desk seething with emotion, she replayed last night's conversation in her head repeatedly.

"So what did your wife say when you said that you would be leaving her for me?" she asked Carlos while they sat drinking in the back of a cocktail bar after work.

He looked down at his drink.

"Well?"

"I...I haven't told her." Recovering his confidence, he looked her in the eye. "Look, Maria, what we have is great. It works for us both. Why do we have to spoil it?"

"Spoil it! You said you wanted to be with me all the time. Oh, I get it, you only say that when you wanna get in my pants. How dumb am I. Well, it might work for you, but it doesn't for me. It's over Carlos. I'm not just here for your sexual gratification. Goodbye."

She got to her feet and stormed out of the bar, leaving him confused. He thought she was happy with the luxury gifts and nights away. It had certainly cost him enough, the Gucci purses and Louboutin shoes, trips to Palm Springs and Vegas, even one to Maui and a promise of a visit to Paris in the spring.

Maria's phone rang, jolting her back to the present.

"Could you step in here for a moment?" On his desk stood photos of his wife and kids, the loving family man upholding the values on which he was seeking reelection. "Take a seat."

She sat down opposite him not uttering a word but throwing him an inscrutable look.

"Given how you feel about our situation, I think it would be best if you quit. You can count on a good reference, of course."

"Not so fast Carlos-"

"It's Governor from now on."

"It's asshole as far as I'm concerned. If you

dare fire me, I'll go to the press and tell them about our affair. I'm not the one who should suffer for this."

"You don't scare me, Maria. I'll deny it, say it's the desperate act of a woman who's no good at her job. You won't get a decent job in this State if you cross me, you better believe that."

They glared at each other like boxers in a ring. Carlos took a deep breath, he needed to calm things down. If she didn't keep quiet, his wife would probably leave him, and he certainly didn't want that. Maria had been fun but he didn't love her. She wasn't worth wrecking his marriage for.

"Listen, Maria, I don't want us to part on bad terms. Let's not ruin our memories of the good times we've had together. You can stay for up to a month. That should give you enough time to find something else."

Maria restrained herself, she would say nothing further for now but she would get even. Why should her career be sacrificed on the altar of his inability to maintain a working relationship with her? He would rue the day he had met Maria Fuentes, she would make sure of it.

She returned to her office. The phone rang, it was the White House, the President for the

Governor. What could he be calling about? Her curiosity was thwarted when Carlos took the call on his private line. But Carlos didn't remember to make his next call on a private line, and Maria was listening in.

"Hey, Seth, I just had Ted on the line. He asked if I could update you. The pipeline construction is ahead of schedule. Water could be flowing from Canada in little over a year, well before we run out. Looks like it'll work out fine after all. The public will never know how close we came to disaster."

"That's great news," the Governor of California replied.

"Yeah ain't it just, saved our asses that's for damn sure. But we're not out of the woods yet. Ted says the Canadian Prime Minister will be in a shit load of trouble when news gets out that he agreed to our demands so if it's finished before the news breaks it will make life a lot easier for everyone."

"Okay, got it. Shall I let Carl know?"

"Yeah, that'd be great."

"Talk soon, buddy."

Maria sat quietly digesting what she'd overheard. Carlos talking to the Governor of California who was to speak to the Governor of

Nevada. They'd been in contact a lot these past few months, but she had thought it was to sort out when and where they would next be meeting up for a game of golf. Water running out, a pipeline from Canada...this was something she could use. Something she could use to give Carlos what he deserved, and probably make money from too. Her frown was gone. She had never expected revenge would be so quick and so easy.

That night, Maria stayed late in the office going through endless computer files, searching for more information. She found nothing but there were still the Governor's private files, the ones that she didn't have access to.

Arriving home, she put a frozen mac and cheese into the microwave and poured a glass of red wine. Later, after another glass of red, she plucked up the courage to phone her former boyfriend.

"Hi, Wayne."

"Maria?"

"Yeah, it's me."

"What the hell do you want?" His voice was gruff.

"I'm working on something. I could do with a little help. There'd be money in it for you. Can you meet me down at the Jalapeño bar in about an hour?"

"Okay, I'll come but there better be big bucks in it for me."

"There will be."

Maria was nervous as she drove to the bar. She had taken care to keep her whereabouts secret from Wayne since they'd split over a year ago, but she needed to hack into those files and he was the only person she knew who could help her do that.

The bar was dim inside, its lighting low, which probably appealed to its clientele, a mixed bag of hustlers and drifters.

In the half-light, Maria saw Wayne seated in a back corner nursing a bourbon. He had the same handsome, rugged look which had first attracted her, his mean streak hidden beneath an alluring smile and brought out by liquor. She'd foolishly agreed to forgive the first beating after his tears and promises of how it would never happen again, but it did and she had ended their relationship shortly afterward.

"Thanks for coming, Wayne," she said as she sat down.

"Where are you hanging out these days, Maria? Why'd you just up and leave without a word?"

"We both know why, Wayne. Can we please not go there? If you don't want to help, I'll go now."

"Okay, tell me what this is all about."

"I need your help to access some computer files in the Governor's office. I'm pretty sure he's up to something the press would pay big money to get their hands on, and I'm happy to split it with you fifty-fifty."

"Jeez Maria, don't you know that'd be a felony?"

"If he's concealing what I think he is, the authorities aren't going to be interested in going after us. They'll have a lot more important issues to focus on."

"So just what would I be looking for exactly if I agreed to take this on?"

She lowered her voice to almost a whisper.

"I overheard a call today between our Governor and the Governor of California. It seems they know there's a big problem coming with water, or the lack of it, that we're gonna run out of the stuff pretty soon. The federal government has strong-armed Canada into letting us pump their water down here. They're building a pipeline but it's all being kept secret. The President himself called the Governor to update him. You'd be looking for anything to do with that."

"That sounds like heavy shit, and dangerous too. I'd need something up front."

"How's five hundred sound?"

He snorted with derision.

"You gotta be kidding me. Ten grand minimum or it ain't happening."

That was a lot for Maria but she could pawn some of the gifts which the Governor had lavished on her, and who knows how much she would make out of breaking this story to the media. She had already fantasized about her fifteen minutes of fame. Talk shows, exclusive deals for the rights to her story, maybe moving back to Mexico and buying a villa in Puerto Vallarta or Los Cabos.

"It's a deal."

"I'll need your password to the network."

"Won't that implicate me?"

"Not the way I do it."

"I'll send it to your cell. How long's it gonna take?"

"I don't know, it could be days or weeks."

"Well, you'll need to hurry. I won't be

working there much longer."

"Oh, the Governor got tired of screwing you and needs you out, is that it?"

"That's none of your business," responded Maria tersely. "I think we're done here."

She got up to go and began to walk away.

"The money?" he called after her.

"I'll get it to you by the end of the week."

CHAPTER 15

A couple of weeks after their meeting at the Jalapeño came the call Maria had been waiting for.

"I got the stuff you wanted. Can you meet me after work at the Holiday Inn off I-10 on the way to Tucson?"

"Yeah, what time?"

"Seven o'clock, and wear something pretty. I might buy you dinner for old time's sake."

Great, thought Maria, he wanted more than money. Still, she was smarter now and knew how to handle him. Wayne was waiting in the lobby.

"I got us reservations," he announced proudly. "The steak here's real good."

She forced herself to smile. Wayne looked the loser he always was. Dressed in jeans, a western shirt and cowboy boots, his idea of fashion but which didn't attract her in the slightest. What had she ever seen in him? He had no interest in the finer things of life as his dining choice demonstrated. Maria inhaled deeply, it was going to be a long evening.

"I'm really not hungry. Do you mind if we just sit at the bar," she said, hoping that way it would be over more quickly.

"Sure, I'm cool with that, and when we're done why don't we go up to the room I got and use the mini bar. Maybe fool around a little for old times sake," he smirked.

"What did you get?" she asked quickly changing the subject.

"It's all just like you said. Seems they found out a few months ago that their data was total bullshit. The state of Arizona, not to mention California and Nevada, is right on track to run out of water in less than two years. There won't be enough left to support more than a few thousand of us, and the Apache and Navajo will get it all back. I sent what you need by email. I hid the password, on my dick," he laughed. "What are you having to drink?"

"A double vodka." She would need a strong drink to get through this.

They drank mainly in silence. He had no conversation, or none that she enjoyed. While he talked, her mind wandered. The media would pay a lot for this. It had to be dynamite, especially with an election this year. He drank heavily and was starting to become incoherent and, hopefully, incapable.

"Why don't we go to the room now and play hunt the password?" she suggested, forcing a smile.

"Sure thing, doll." He gave her a wink that did anything but seduce her, followed by a loud burp.

Wayne walked unsteadily with her to the elevator and along the corridor to the room. Once inside, he promptly fell face down on the bed. Maria smiled, the pill she'd dropped in his drink at the bar had worked. Reverse date rape. You go girl, she congratulated herself. Now all she had to do was find the password. She tried his pockets but without success.

Perhaps he really had been serious. Maria pushed his body with all her might to roll him over onto his back and undressed him. He hadn't been joking. He actually had a post-it attached to his penis. It said, predictably, "BlowMe2Night!"

Quickly she accessed his email on her cell and tried the password. It worked. What a dumb ass he was but that no longer mattered, she had all that she needed. Maria emptied some liquor from the mini bar down the toilet. Then she scattered the bottles around the room and messed up the bed. When he woke up with a sore head, she wanted him to think he'd had a good time.

Maria drove back to her ranch house and downloaded the information. She also printed off a copy, and next morning deposited it in her safe box at the bank. Once back home again, she rang the offices of the state's biggest newspaper.

"Good morning, I need to speak with your editor. I have some really important news he will want to be the first to have."

"He doesn't take calls. Can you tell me what it's about? I could see if one of our staff reporters is available," responded a woman's voice.

Maria wasn't going to be brushed off with some rookie reporter. She wanted someone who would know how to make maximum impact.

"Look, I really don't have time to waste here. If you don't put me through right now I'll be on the phone to your competitor, and when your boss finds out that you blew his chance of getting the biggest news story of the year, you sure as hell won't be up for employee of the month."

"Please hold and I'll see what I can do."

A few moments later, a man came on the line.

"Hi, it's Hank Dubois here. I understand you

have the news story of the year for us," he said in a tone which betrayed his belief that she didn't.

"Yes I do, but it's not something I wish to discuss on the phone."

"Well, can you at least give me some indication of what it's about. I'm sure you'll appreciate we get a lot of calls every day from people making all kinds of claims."

"Let me just say I worked in the Governor's office until recently, and I have information on a cover up that will have very serious consequences for him, not to mention everyone who lives in this State."

Hank's interest was rising, maybe she wasn't the usual nutcase.

"Where do you want to meet?"

"The Skydeck at five is good for me."

"Okay, that'll work. How will I recognize you?"

"I'll be in a green dress."

Hank got there first and chose a table. It was a pleasant evening, about seventy degrees, a refreshing change from the suffocating heat of summer. Winter was without doubt the best season in Phoenix, a time when you could appreciate the outdoors without being roasted alive and feel superior to the rest of the country, most of which was in the freezer.

Maria arrived fifteen minutes late. Hank made a hesitant wave with his hand as she walked in looking for him. He had curly brown hair almost down to his shoulders. Probably still only in his late twenties, not the senior reporter she'd wanted but at least likely to have some experience.

"Hi, I'm Hank," he said standing up to shake her hand.

"Good to meet you, Hank. I'm Maria."

"What can I get you?"

"I'll have a Cosmo."

Hank got the waiter's attention and ordered a Cosmopolitan for her and a Mojito for himself. They chatted superficially about the weather and the Phoenix traffic until the waiter returned with their drinks.

"So you have the story of the year for me?"

"If I told you that the Governor knows that our water supplies are going to get so low that in a couple of years our economy here in the Southwest will no longer be able to function but he has chosen not to tell us, wouldn't that be the story of the year?"

"Yes, I guess it would."

"And if I told you the President knows too, and that he has done a secret deal with Canada to take their water and a pipeline is being built to get it down here."

"That would certainly be some story. But what proof do you have? I don't mean to be rude but it does kinda sound like a movie, not real life."

"I have emails to and from the Governor to back it all up."

"I'll need to see those."

"You shall, as soon as we cut a deal."

"A deal?" said Hank, feigning surprise.

"Yes, a deal. I'm not doing all this for free. I'll give you exclusivity but I want a million dollars."

Hank exhaled. "Wow, that's some serious dough. I don't know if we can pay you-"

"If it's more than you can afford, I'll go elsewhere."

"I'm sure you won't need to do that but I'll need some time to get this approved," said Hank quickly backtracking.

The newspaper would probably only pay half that amount at most, but he was sure he could talk her down. There would be huge profit, not to mention prestige, in being the first to break the story and to be the one with exclusive access to her.

"You can have a week but no longer. Here's my number." She handed him a small folded piece of paper taken from her clutch and took a quick sip of her cocktail. "Thanks for the drink. I need to be going now. I'll look forward to hearing from you."

"I'll be in touch real soon," promised Hank, standing up as she stood to leave.

He watched Maria go. She certainly was driving a hard bargain but that didn't matter. If what she claimed was true and she had the evidence to back it up this would be big. No more chasing down inconsequential local stories for him. If he nailed this one, he would be a national name, headhunted by the New York Times or Washington Post. Maybe after years of drifting from newspaper to newspaper all around the Southwest, he'd finally hit the jackpot.

Hank left what remained of his drink, paid the waiter, and drove back to the office as fast as he could. He needed to speak to the editor urgently.

CHAPTER 16

It was the first visit of Canadian Prime Minister, Michael Beaumont, to Washington since his agreement to allow his country's water to be taken south. The President welcomed him effusively, but Michael couldn't help feeling like someone on the outside looking in. He was a bystander. His country played, and always would play, second fiddle to its neighbor.

Alone together after the obligatory photo call, they sat in the White House library. Michael glanced up at the picture of George Washington on the wall. Washington's painter had given him an almost supercilious look. Was the nation's first President smirking at him and the change in fortunes? Two hundred and fifty years ago, America was a minor power on the edge of civilization. And a vulnerable one, as Britain had reminded her in 1814 attacking from Canada and burning down the Capitol and the White House in retaliation for American incursions into Canada. Now Canada was the minor power, unable to escape the orbit of the world's preeminent military machine. Michael could do little but pay homage at the court of the great chief.

"I'm glad to finally have the opportunity to thank you in person, Michael. You've shown you're a true friend who we can count on in time of need. America won't forget that."

"I'd say you're welcome but I don't think we had much choice in the matter. Still, I'm grateful you're upholding your part of the bargain. Your speech against the independence of Quebec certainly helped. The margin against was much higher than I dared hope. But now I need you to deliver on your promise about territorial waters in the Arctic."

"I certainly intend to do that, you have my word. I've instructed my people to reach agreement by the end of the month. But I need to ask you to keep it under wraps until after the election."

"What if you lose?" asked Michael.

"If you've been following the news, you'll know that's most unlikely. The Republicans are tearing themselves apart in the primaries, and the polls show whichever candidate they choose, I'm a long way out in front."

"Voters are fickle. What if news gets out?"

"I'm confident it won't, not until the pipeline's ready. My people have got excellent monitoring in place. They're confident we can prevent any leaks, if you'll excuse the pun." Ted Jackson laughed at his own joke. "If news did get out we've got agreed scripts, right?"

"We have but politically I expect to be finished."

"You need to be more positive than that, Michael. You've a good story to tell, we both have. Going public would have caused a serious economic crisis, throwing millions out of work. And look what you've achieved for Canada – squashing independence for Quebec and US acceptance of your claims in the Arctic. Yeah, the first few days will be rough but once folks stop and think about it rationally, they'll rally behind you."

"It would be nice to think that's the way my fellow countrymen will see it, but there's something deep in the Canadian mindset about our water and keeping it just that, our water. When do you expect the pipeline to be operational?"

"In less than twelve months. They're making good progress. You probably know already that the construction of the pumping station at Lake Athabasca is well underway. Some of the pipeline construction is proving harder than expected but it's still on schedule."

"That's good to know. I guess we should get our people in so we can get through our agenda."

CHAPTER 17

Angel had been more restless than usual since returning from his summer trip to South Dakota. He'd abandoned plans to start school in the fall. The idea of trying to be a white collar worker wasn't for him. He couldn't make a difference playing with numbers on a computer and wasn't cut out for an office job. His jail time would probably kill any job application anyway.

Angel's conundrum was he didn't feel part of America, yet he wasn't part of the Apache nation either. He needed to have a plan if his desire to make a difference to the life of Native Americans was ever going to amount to anything but he didn't know where to start.

Angel had at least decided that come June he would go visit Mingan who he'd met at the powwow in South Dakota. Having never left the USA before, he wanted to broaden both his horizons and his mind. The Apache had migrated from what is now western Canada several hundred years ago and spoke a related Athabaskan language so ethnically they were linked with Mingan's ancestors.

He hoped Paige too might still be up in Canada at the time of his visit. They messaged regularly and he felt drawn to her even though they'd never met. She seemed the kind of person who would understand him. No one else did.

Until his trip, he would continue staying at his mom's house. They didn't get along; she didn't relate to his whole heritage thing, and wanted him to get some direction in his life. Angel had now switched to night shifts. He could earn more that way, and it also had the advantage for him that they rarely saw each other.

She'd left her job at the Governor's office and taken one at a local car dealership. It seemed an odd choice to him but she claimed the stress had been too much and, after all, she'd reminded him, who was he to question people on their career choices when he flipped burgers for a living.

One Thursday in late winter, Angel finished work around six in the morning as usual and drove back to his mother's house. When he rounded the corner to her street, the scene unfolding before his eyes caused him to brake hard and turn off his headlights. From the light cast by the streetlights, he could see about two hundred feet away four police cars and cops crouched down behind them, their firearms pointing toward the house. Two other officers with guns at the ready stood either side of the front door. One shouted out something and shot at the lock as they both forced open the door and disappeared inside.

Angel's natural instinct was to run down the street to protect his mother but he held back. Only the evening before when he'd passed through the kitchen heading out to work, she had stopped him.

"Hey, Angel, wait up. I need to talk to you for a moment."

"I don't need another lecture. This is my life."

It seemed whenever they spoke these days, she would do nothing but criticize him.

"Angel, my life could be in danger."

That got his attention.

"What are you talking about?"

"I have some information that others will want to stop becoming public knowledge, and I don't know just how far they're willing to go to achieve that."

"Are you breaking the law?"

"Theoretically maybe but it's a matter of huge public interest."

"So what is it?"

"You don't need to know. If you did, you might become a target. Here's the code to my bank deposit box. Take it." She handed him a piece of paper. "Keep it with you and if something happens to me, open the box and decide for yourself what to do with what you find. But above all, stay safe. It's not worth risking your life over."

"So why should it be worth yours? Mom, you're scaring me."

"It's something I wanted to do, something I've already done. Hey, you better get going or you'll be late for work," she said as though everything was as normal as it had been before her revelation.

Uncharacteristically, she came over to him and kissed him on the cheek, and for once he didn't cringe or move away but hugged her tightly.

"Just don't do anything crazy. Promise me, okay?"

"I won't. You're a good kid, Angel." She saved her tears until after he had gone.

Earlier that day when she'd chased Hank for an update, she was told that he no longer worked at the newspaper. Checking the internet, she got goose bumps when she found a news report of how a "promising young journalist, Hank Dubois" had been killed in a car crash three days ago. Coincidence it could be but she didn't believe so.

Angel slid down low in his seat. Shots rang out. His world stopped. His mother. They had to have shot his mother. He remained where he was, paralyzed by shock and horror. Only moments later with lights flashing, an ambulance appeared. It must have been waiting close by. It couldn't have arrived so quickly otherwise. Soon afterward, Angel's worst fears were confirmed when a stretcher on which lay a body covered by a sheet was wheeled down the driveway toward the ambulance.

His nightmare intensified as a voice yelled at him.

"Hey, you! Get out of the car with your hands up."

A cop was hurrying toward him followed by another. Angel switched the engine on and began reversing fast. The sound of gunfire erupted again. A bullet hit the windshield, shattering it into hundreds of tiny cracks. The glass deflected the bullet and it missed Angel. He could hear policemen shouting while they ran to their vehicles. Rounding the corner, Angel spun the wheels to turn, hit the gas, and sped down the street, bouncing off a couple of parked cars as he did so.

He couldn't see where he was going. Grabbing an unopened can of Coke resting in the cup holder, he used it to punch out broken glass from the windshield until he could see the road ahead. A cool wind hit his face. In his rearview mirror, he could see the cops in hot pursuit.

Soon he was out of town, but they were gaining on him. Angel pulled over. Taking the can of drink, he jumped out and began running away from the highway as dawn was breaking.

Angel didn't look behind him but he heard the police cars skidding to a halt. His heart pounding, he threw himself behind a rock as bullets ricocheted off the ground near him. Noticing that he was only a few feet from a canyon about six feet deep, Angel ran, jumping down into it and following its twisting course. The cops did the same. The canyon led toward the slopes of mountains about a mile away.

Although every sinew in his body was strained to the limit and the pulsating in his temples was so loud he thought he could run no further, Angel willed himself to keep going, thinking of how his grandmother would have urged him on, reminding him of how much more his ancestors had endured. Once amongst the rocks and crevices of those mountains, he could hide and not be discovered. It was in his blood. No one could conceal themselves better than an Apache.

He reached the slopes at the end of the canyon. On and up Angel went, staying behind boulders as much as possible. The rising sun now cast a bright early morning light of searchlight intensity. The mountains had changed from a dark purple hue to a bright sandy color, but Angel didn't have time to appreciate the beauty of the moment.

The occasional shot pierced the still air but they all went wide of him. Fast and nimble, Angel had a good lead. The police, not used to this terrain, failed to close the gap. The route he was following went around a corner and out of sight of his pursuers. Above him, he saw an obvious way to ascend. To his left was the narrowest of ledges, not even wide enough to stand on properly with a sheer drop of over one hundred feet beneath it. That was the route he chose. They wouldn't think he'd gone in that direction.

First, however, Angel went up the path above him, leaving tracks in the dust until he reached rocks he could have scrambled over without leaving footprints. He gulped down some Coke and threw the empty can up the slope, another indication to those hunting him that he had continued climbing. Then he carefully retraced his steps, descending backward, and standing in the same footprints left in the dust.

When Angel reached the narrow ledge, he was forced to stand on tiptoes. With his body pressed flat against the rock face and his arms outstretched, he grabbed every meager handhold he could. He shuffled nervously along the ledge not knowing if it would lead anywhere. Stones and dirt fell away beneath his feet. Angel's face was pressed so close to the rock that he couldn't look down or up. He knew that if he fell he would die or be found lying injured by the police who would doubtless put a bullet through him.

His arms and legs began shaking involuntarily. Angel felt his ability to hold on in this constricted position slipping away from him. His muscles ached and his hands were now cut and bleeding from pushing them into gaps that weren't large enough but gave some much needed stability.

At one point, his right leg gave way. He scraped skin from his face as he slid down the rock face, halting in a semi-crouching position. If he didn't get back up quickly, his center of gravity would soon pull him backward into a fall. Carefully, Angel moved his head and body upward to regain a standing position and continued. To his great relief, not long afterward he reached a narrow crevice in the rock face into which he was able to squeeze sideways. It rose twenty feet above him until it closed. He couldn't turn or sit but he didn't care, he was just glad to be off that ledge and in the shade out of the sun.

Finally feeling safer and no longer focused solely on his own survival, he relived the horror of this morning. The grief hit him like a tidal wave. The person who had always been there, who he had taken for granted, baited, ignored, and railed against was no longer. Angel was an orphan now. No parents, no siblings, no family. He let out deep, guttural sobs of hurt and despair.

At some point Angel's tears abated. He had no more. His thoughts turned to why. Why had they killed his mother? What exactly had she known that would make them want to murder her? Was it somehow linked to her old job working for the Governor?

During the rest of the morning and afternoon, he could hear the loud and threatening shuddering of helicopters flying over the area searching for him. When dusk fell, it became quiet. Desperately thirsty, not having had a drink in twelve hours, he needed to get out of here. Emerging carefully from his hiding place, Angel began the long, unwelcome shuffle along the ledge to where he could begin to descend. As he went, he listened for that eerie shaking sound. This was rattlesnake territory and the time of day they would be most active. A snake bite would end his chance of making it out alive.

Making it back to the path down, Angel walked toward the highway and followed it out of sight of passing vehicle lights until he reached the city outskirts. He walked along back streets he knew to his mother's house. It must have been after ten when he got there. The cops had left for the night. Going around the back, he went in through the rear door. He didn't dare to turn on the lights. In the kitchen, he guzzled glass after glass of water to quench his thirst. He wanted to shower but it was too dangerous to stay that long.

Angel knew where his mother hid the money he was going to need. With trepidation, he entered his mother's bedroom. Nothing could have prepared him for what he saw. The moon cast a sinister light across the room. Her bedding was pulled back. On the wall, smeared blood ran in parallel lines to the floor. He retched at the sight.

An image invaded his mind of her getting out of bed and trying to escape. Shot many times as her killers barged into the room, her bloodied fingers sliding down the wall while she fell dying to the ground. Angel became unsteady, overwhelmed with emotion and nausea but he needed to get away from here as quickly as possible if he was to evade capture.

Taking a book that he knew wasn't really a book from her bookshelf, he opened it. Hollow, it contained a large wad of cash which he took. Next, he went to his room to get his gun. It had gone. From the open drawers and scattered clothes, it was clear the cops must have gone through his things. Returning to the kitchen, Angel took her car keys from a hook on the wall and went into the garage using the connecting door from the house.

Thankfully, her SUV was still there. He listened for noise from outside. There was none. Pressing the automatic garage door opener, he anxiously watched the door rise. The street outside was deserted. He reversed out, activated the control for the door to close again, and drove away.

On the other side of town, Angel checked in at a cheap motel. He showered quickly and then sat on the bed surfing through the TV channels until he hit upon a news item about his mother's shooting. A reporter stood outside their home from earlier that day, explaining that a drugs bust had ended in a shootout and the unfortunate death of Maria Fuentes. The cops had now launched a manhunt for Angel, her son, who managed to escape. The police claimed his mother pulled a gun when they tried to arrest her. He knew that to be an outright lie. She didn't have a gun or even know how to shoot.

Angel went out to get a burger and brought it back to the room. He was hungry but in such turmoil he couldn't eat more than a couple of mouthfuls. Eventually he fell asleep, spending a tormented night and waking frequently, his whole being aching from his loss. Before dawn, he was wide awake and his mind had cleared.

Early that morning, he drove to his mother's bank. Using the code on the piece of paper which she'd given him the night before her murder, he opened her deposit box. Inside was a large envelope which he took. Back in his dowdy room, he ripped it open and pulled out the papers inside. The first was a handwritten letter from his mother.

"My dear Angel,

If you are reading this, I am probably in jail or maybe worse. If I am still alive, please don't try to see me. And don't go back home. They will think you know what I know and come after you. Leave Arizona as quickly as you can.

Unbelievable as it sounds, the Governor all the way up to the President are involved in a massive cover up to keep from us all that water supplies are now so low that life here will soon be unsustainable so they are planning to take water from Canada. Read the papers with this note and you'll get the picture.

If you can use this information without endangering yourself in any way, then do so but DO NOT take any risks. You have your whole life in front of you.

Never forget I love you and always will. Be true to yourself.

Mom."

Angel's vision misted with tears. Wiping his eyes, he read the hard copy emails. Pipelines to take water from Great Bear, Great Slave, and Athabasca lakes in Canada to the US, a plan to keep it secret for as long as possible. While he sat there stunned by what he had read, the enormity of it all began to sink in. This information was power. Power to change his life. Power to change the status quo.

Always an outsider in both his father's world and his mother's, never properly part of either one, this gave him the chance to become an insider, a hero amongst the Apache. If he could stop the pipelines, Americans would be forced to pack up and leave the Southwest in their millions for lack of water.

Angel thought for a while. He would visit Mingan. This was way too big to deal with alone.

Angel knew the geography now. After returning from the powwow, he'd googled where Mingan lived and the country around there. Mingan wasn't so far from Lake Athabasca. Paige too might be able to help. This was exactly the kind of thing which she'd been warning about.

He and Mingan would go to the lake and check out what was happening and then, when he broke the news, he would be believed, not dismissed as some crazy person. Once word got out, there would surely be panic and huge political repercussions. The whole pipeline plan might just collapse, and he would be able to prove his mother had been murdered because she'd found out about it.

Mingan was off the grid, without cell or internet, but he could contact Paige. He knew better than to message her about the cover up. The government was probably monitoring his communications, and even if they weren't spying on him directly they would surely be picking up any chatter about the issue. He used the motel phone to call her. It was a risk but hopefully less than using his cell. He would be out of here soon.

"Hi, Paige. It's me, Angel."

"Hi! Well, this is a surprise."

"Look, I don't have time to talk right now but

I'm coming up to Canada. I should be there in two or three days. It'd be great to meet up if you're around."

"That'd be awesome. I can't wait to meet you. I'm in Saskatoon right now. I'll send you directions."

"No, I've lost my cell. Just give me your address, I'll find you."

He smiled when he put the phone down, the first smile which had appeared on his face since his mother's death. Angel's inconsequential life was about to change.

He then went to the front desk to use their photocopier.

"That'll be five dollars for the first five pages and fifty cents a page after that," said the gum-chewing receptionist with a ring through her nose.

She held out her hand for the papers.

"They're personal. I'd like to copy them myself."

She threw him a look of annoyance that he would question her trustworthiness.

"Okay, you can come back here and do it."

He returned to his room and put the copies in the envelope. Out in the parking lot, he threw the envelope onto the passenger seat and placed the originals underneath it.

CHAPTER 18

A few hours later on the other side of the country in New York, night was falling and the temperature was dropping rapidly. The sidewalks were almost deserted except for the homeless, bedding down for a bitterly cold night which would seem unending.

Ethan was sitting at the bar in the Royalton Hotel in midtown Manhattan. There on business, he felt like celebrating. Today he'd won an important new client, and an hour ago his boss had called to tell him he was being promoted to Vice President.

On returning to the hotel, he called an old flame who worked in New York, and upgraded to a suite with one of their large round tubs and an open fire, which was being lit while he drank. He was on his second cocktail waiting for his date to arrive. The concierge had managed to get him a table in one of the city's top new restaurants in SoHo, good enough he hoped to entice his date back to the hotel for the night.

As usual the place was buzzing, everyone having a good time after a hard day at the office. The subdued lighting, giant double-sided gas effect fire encased in glass, and the brown and gold palette made for a warm and comforting atmosphere.

Ethan didn't pay much attention when a man sat down next to him and shouted at the bartender to try and attract his attention.

"What you gotta do to get served around here?" he said turning to Ethan.

"They're busy." Ethan didn't bother to look at the guy, he wasn't in the mood for conversation with a stranger, especially this one.

"It's Ethan, right?"

He had Ethan's attention now. The man didn't look like one of the regular Royalton crowd. Ethan guessed he must be close to sixty. Unkempt, his white shirt was no longer white, his tie had a large stain on it, his jacket was from twenty years ago, and by the look of him, he hadn't shaved that day. His body aroma wasn't too good either.

"How do you know my name?" demanded Ethan.

"I know a lot about you. Where you live, where you work, where you hang out. That's what I get paid for."

"Get paid for? Just who the hell are you?"

"Hey calm down, pal, unless you wanna draw attention to yourself. I have some friends who want some information. They'll pay a lot of money for it."

"You can't be serious."

"Angharad Jones, Secretary of State, that is. Know her?" Ethan didn't answer. "Well of course you do, you're screwing her. My friends just need some information as to what she's been up to with her clandestine trips to Canada. I'm sure you know her inside out, literally."

He made an unpleasant laughing sound that seemed to come from his nostrils rather than his mouth.

"I don't know what your game is, but you better beat it fast before I have you thrown out."

"I guess you could do that but before you do, does the name Cristina Lopez mean anything to you? I've been talking with her. I think she might be willing to go to court."

Ethan became rigid as though a ghost had passed right through him. He'd never expected to hear that name again.

It had taken the private detective a long time to find something which he could use to get Ethan to be motivated to give him the information he wanted, months of painstaking investigation. His clients were impatient, they needed an answer. He'd told them they would only need to hold on a little longer, he would get them what they wanted.

"I can see you need some time to think, time to reflect. You wouldn't want that information falling into the wrong hands. You're in PR, your clients wouldn't like it. Don't wreck your career, son, just when it's taking off. Here's my number, give me a call tomorrow. Guess I'm not gonna get that beer after all."

He got down from his bar stool, leaving Ethan reeling from their encounter. Before he had time to process, Selina arrived. Although she looked as gorgeous as ever, dressed in a body hugging black dress, her usually long flowing blond hair up in an elegant chignon, and smelled so enticingly feminine, the evening passed him by in a haze. She chatted throughout dinner but he found it hard to focus on conversation.

Ethan kept thinking of that fateful evening in his last year of college, partying with his football buddies at a nightclub in Boston. He'd hit on Cristina and danced the night away with her. She willingly jumped in the cab back to college with him and went up to his room for coffee. They'd kissed but when he'd gone further she'd resisted. He told her she wanted it, despite her denials and took what he wanted by force. She ran out crying but he didn't care. To him, she was only a slutty waitress from downtown. If she complained no one was going to believe her story against a Harvard student.

He was thus caught by surprise the next morning when the police arrived and took him in for questioning. They told him he was likely to be charged with rape. Ethan was facing an end to his career before it even started, years in jail and life as a sex offender. However, the next day they let him go. She'd dropped her allegation, probably not wanting to go through a public court hearing of hostile questioning and having to relive the night. Ethan had always thought that was an end of it. Somehow that low life old man had found out about it and was threatening to rake the whole thing up again.

Ethan and Selina were sitting in the round tub luxuriating in the warm water and scented bubbles. Candles gave a soft glow. It should have been the perfect evening. She was pulling him toward her. He fought to focus.

"What's wrong, Ethan? You've been distant all night, and now I'm throwing myself at you and your mind is somewhere else."

"I'm sorry, I can't stop thinking about work. Can we do this some other time?"

"I'll go," she said, sounding hurt.

Ethan tried to sleep. It was nearly morning before he did. When he awoke, he knew he had no choice.

"It's Ethan. I'll do it."

"Good. They've authorized me to pay you ten thousand when you give us something useful."

"It may take a while." Ethan was hoping to buy enough time to never have to do anything.

"You got two weeks. If you don't give me something by then, your boss might just get to hear about your past."

"But-"

The line went dead.

CHAPTER 19

Instead of heading north to Canada, Angel drove south-east. After a few hours, he reached the San Carlos reservation. Established in 1872 and referred to as 'Hell's forty acres', it hadn't changed much since then, a dry and barren place offering dust, flies, and sweltering temperatures. It was another place of poverty with rampant unemployment and widespread deprivation. A casino had brought some work but not much.

Angel was transported back to his childhood. It must have been almost fifteen years since he last visited. He thought of his grandmother and how he used to bounce up and down with excitement in the back of the car as he arrived to spend a few weeks of his school summer vacation. He pulled in at the general store.

"I need to see the tribal elders," he told the woman behind the counter.

"Why?" asked a man standing nearby. He was elderly but remained tall and sinewy. With gray hair in two braids, he wore a checked shirt and jeans. His obsidian eyes looked Angel up and down.

“I have some important information they need to know.”

“You ain’t from round here, but you look like us,” said the man, a note of curiosity in his voice.

“That’s because I am one of you. I haven’t been here since I was a kid. My father was Tarak and my grandmother Nascha. I’m Angel.”

The man grinned at him in recognition.

“Last time I saw you, you were just a kid. You lived in Phoenix with your mother if I recall correctly. Come with me.”

He led Angel across the street and down a dirt track to a modest home. He knocked on the door. Another man of similar age opened it and stepped outside.

“This here is Nascha’s grandson, Angel. You remember her. She passed about ten years back. He ain’t been here for years. He says he has some important information for us.

“Well, you’ve sure grown,” said the other man. “What is it that you have to tell us?”

“Okay, this might sound a little crazy but it’s the truth. My mom worked in the Governor’s office. She got hold of information about how the State is gonna run out of water real soon. The government's hushed it all up and is taking water from Canada, building a pipeline and bringing it down here. Anyway, it seems they found out she knew and they had her shot." His voice began to break. The two men looked at him sympathetically while he fought to recover his composure. "She left me some papers, hardcopy emails that prove what's going on. I took a copy. I want you to have them in case anything happens to me."

He offered them a large brown envelope. They didn't take it.

"And what is it you want us to do with that exactly?" asked the man from the store.

"Can't you see? This is the biggest opportunity for us since the first settlers arrived. Without water, the white man's history in the Southwest. We could get our land back if we stop this pipeline. I'm going up to Canada to meet with our brothers there, check out what's happening before I go to the media. If you don't hear from me in a month, you can assume I'm dead or in jail, and you can make the whole thing public."

The two men spoke in Apache. Angel only understood a few words, not enough to get any sense of what they were saying. His grandmother had tried to teach him the language without success. Apache is a tonal language, something which was completely alien to him, and which he'd never mastered. The man from the store spoke.

"Look son, you do what you gotta do but we don't want to get involved. We've plenty of trouble to deal with in our own backyard. The lake here is almost out of water. We don't get people coming to fish no more. The Coolidge dam is just about empty. We need that water from Canada."

"You cannot be serious! Stopping this is the best thing to happen to us since Goyakla had the US cavalry disappearing up their own asses trying to find him."

"We've given you our decision. You need to go."

"Oh, I'm going all right, and you can get back to being good 'Injuns' for the tourists!"

Angel kicked the dust in frustration and walked away. To hell with them, he thought, I will do this thing by myself if I have to. Angel didn't understand their submissiveness or lack of vision. For hundreds of years they had lived as they wanted to, and yet in only a generation in the 1800s their way of life had been extinguished. Now there was a chance that the white man's insatiable demand for water, his taking from mother earth without a thought for the consequences, would be his undoing. Without a lifeline from Canada, millions would have to leave. Once more the Apache would be able to wander freely across the Southwest and reclaim what had been taken from them.

Angel took a circuitous route north, not wanting to drive through Arizona and face a greater risk of being caught. He drove east into New Mexico and up to Taos where he found a motel for the night. The next day, he drove into Colorado heading for Durango. Stopping there to buy the winter gear he would need, he then headed west for Utah. He was fortunate that the highways weren't closed with snow as they often could be at this time of year.

In the afternoon near Moab, he saw a sign to Dead Horse Point and took it. Angel had heard of this place and wanted to visit it. Parking, he walked to the lookout. He had it all to himself. In the last couple of days he had driven through some amazing landscapes which made his spirit soar, however this was surely the pinnacle.

On the horizon, stood snow covered mountains. In front of him the ground fell away abruptly. Millions of years of erosion had created deep winding canyons in the mesas. Two thousand feet below, the Colorado River flowed flexuous and muddy green, heading for the dams of Arizona and Nevada.

But the once mighty river had become a shadow of its former self, climate change drastically reducing its flow. Farther south, man had literally drained it dry. Where once there had been a delta in Mexico as the river reached the ocean and discharged into the Sea of Cortez, there was no longer any water at all. The river now ended in a whimper, just south of the border with Mexico in a scum of chemicals and garbage.

The sun was setting, partly obscured by charcoal colored clouds, edged in gold against a powder blue sky. Angel stood there a long time, well after the sun dipped below the horizon. He wanted to stay in the moment as long as possible. Despite the cold, he felt safe here. What the future would bring he didn't know, but what he did know was that people were willing to kill for the information he had.

Two days later found Angel in eastern Montana, driving through a blizzard near the US-Canadian border. Thousands of miles in length, it constitutes the longest undefended border on earth. He couldn't use an official border crossing. Angel didn't possess a passport, and even if he had he was probably top of the wanted list.

Pulling off the highway, he turned off his lights. It was late afternoon and the day was fading fast. He could barely make out where he was going in the swirling snowflakes, which had the advantage that it would be difficult for anyone else to see him. Angel bumped along heading north.

He was driving over someone's land, although it was unlikely the owner would be out in this weather. A barbed wire fence blocked his path. Backing up, Angel put his foot on the gas, bringing down a large section of fence as he went through it. Soon he was crossing the "no touch zone", a twenty-foot swathe of nothing running between the two nations to delineate their border. Not long afterward, he reached a highway and turned west. Passing a truck stop, he smiled to see the red and white Canadian flag with its distinctive maple leaf flapping in the wind.

Finding a motel, he called Paige to let her know he would be with her tomorrow. She sounded excited to see him. Angel fell asleep imagining their meeting. He liked the way she looked in her online photos and he was hopeful that they might connect.

CHAPTER 20

Delores Knight was mad, not that she had started the day that way. On the contrary, she'd been in a great mood. She was to meet the President in the Oval Office. This was the moment which she had been imagining in her mind for several weeks now, and preparing for longer than she cared to remember.

Delores represented living proof of the American dream. She'd been raised in South Los Angeles, which wasn't an easy place to thrive in although she had been fortunate to have a supportive family. Delores may have been born disadvantaged but she knew how to dream, and she dreamed big. She burned with ambition. That ambition saw her graduate, get a law degree, and become a partner in a successful law practice in Chicago. It was there that she first met Ted Jackson in the early days of his political career. She too left the firm not many years after him to also move into politics. Jackson by then was an influential figure in the party and helped secure her nomination to run as a Senator for

Illinois, a contest which she'd won.

Her ambition didn't stop there. She wanted to be President, the first African-American woman President. Delores would have liked to run this year, but she knew she couldn't stand against Jackson as incumbent and win. She needed to be patient and bide her time. After all, she had an understanding with Jackson that he would put her on the ticket this fall.

Looking every bit the next Vice President in a designer black top, matching pants, and purple jacket, she strode confidently into the Oval Office. Although now in her late forties, she could have passed for mid-thirties. Her skin was the color of the finest dark chocolate and her complexion flawless. She kept her hair extremely short. She simply didn't have the time to spend washing and drying anything more elaborate but she could carry it off, the style looked great on her. Delores exuded sophistication and intelligence. Someone the electorate could trust to have the skills and experience needed to lead the country if the President should die.

Leading a very disciplined life, she was up at five, in the gym before six, and the office by seven. She rarely relaxed and partied little. Delores was hard on herself, and on others if they didn't meet her high standards. To attain her goals, she knew she would have to be better than any man and accept being judged by more exacting criteria. That was just the way it was and to complain about it would achieve nothing. It remained a man's world. Her single-minded focus on her career left her no time for a partner or a family but she didn't regret it. She was chasing her dream and now could almost reach out and touch it.

Sitting in her office, she replayed in her mind this morning's meeting.

"Hi, Delores, let's sit down over here." The President led her toward the sofas.

He sounded uncharacteristically downbeat, and she noticed that he hadn't yet looked at her directly. Her heartbeat quickened, something wasn't right.

"Delores, let me get straight to the point. I wanted you to be the first to know. I'm not putting you on the ticket."

"What! Why?" This was unexpected and devastating news for her.

"I need someone who can appeal to Latino voters. I don't think that person is you."

"Oh really, and what about the African American vote? Wasn't it me who got them out for you last time?"

"You did and I'm forever grateful, and hope

I can count on you this time. If I can, I'm sure there's a place in my next administration for you. But the simple fact is the Latino vote is more important. They are by far the biggest minority, you know that."

"But we had an understanding, Ted. That job was mine and you know it!"

"And I'm saying you can have another one. You don't need to be Vice President to get the nomination next time around."

"So who is it? Please tell me it's not Linda Hernandez."

"Why? Would that be so bad?"

"Hell yes, she wants the Presidency next time too, and you're giving her the best shot at it."

"Look, Delores, my mind's made up and I'd really appreciate your support."

Delores stood up to go, her brow furrowed with lines of anger.

"I thought I could trust you, Ted. How could I have been so stupid."

She stormed out in a rage, fighting back tears of frustration, and canceled her meetings for the rest of the day.

As the day wore on, she began to calm

down. Who cares if I'm mad or I've been double-crossed? No one, she reasoned, no one but me. No, Delores, don't get mad, get even. Stay in the game, and play like you mean to win.

Delores smiled for the first time since her meeting with the President. She would have her chance. This setback wasn't going to stop her. She had damn well earned this, and no one was going to take it from her. Scrolling through the contacts in her cell phone, she found the one she wanted and pressed call.

CHAPTER 21

Angel arrived at Paige's apartment mid afternoon. She greeted him with a smile and a hug.

"It's so great to finally meet you. Come on in. Can I get you a coffee?"

"Sure, that'd be great," answered Angel sitting down on her sofa. He was nervous and hoped it didn't show. Angel wanted so much for her to like him. She was even lovelier in real life than he had imagined; vivacious, with a sparkle in her eyes.

"Here you go," she said handing the coffee to him as she sat down next to him. "So what is it brings you up here? I thought you'd wait until summer before coming. Travel can be really difficult this time of year."

"I had planned to wait for summer but something has happened, something huge."

Angel proceeded to explain about his mother's death and the pipeline, and showed her the papers he had.

"I'm so sorry, that is just terrible. It's hard to believe, it's like something out of a thriller. But I still don't get what you're up here for right now."

"The guy I met at a powwow in South Dakota last summer lives north of here. I figured I'd go see him and we could check out what is actually going on up there. I want to have something more than these papers before I go to the networks. It would be too easy to be dismissed as some crazy guy with forged papers without any photos as proof."

"Yes, that would get their attention better. I'd really love to help. This is just the kind of thing I've been blogging about. Would you mind if I came along? I've got some great equipment we could use, and funds to pay for the trip. We'll need to fly in, there are no roads up there."

"It could be dangerous. These people are willing to kill to hush this up. I don't want you getting hurt or worse."

"I'm a big girl, Angel. I can look out for myself."

"Okay then, it's a deal," he grinned.

It would be good to have extra help, and he would enjoy being around her. Merely looking at her, or listening to her voice made his heart beat faster.

"Great. Well, you must be hungry. I was gonna order pizza in if that's okay with you. You're welcome to crash on the sofa if you've nowhere else to stay tonight."

"Yes please, I've had my fill of crappy motels these past few days."

"Make yourself at home. Watch TV, take a shower, whatever you want. I need to spend some time chartering a flight. Where is this friend of yours exactly?"

"He told me if I ever came to make my way to the settlement at Cree Lake. He said one of the guys there could take me by dog sled out to his place. He lives out in the bush."

"It's all bush up North. There's really nothing between here and the North Pole, only lakes and forests. You can fly in and out if you can find a frozen lake to land on, of which there are many. Once there, dog sled or snowmobile are the only ways to get around. Do you have the right gear? It'll be super cold."

"Yeah, I got a bunch of stuff on my journey here."

They talked long into the evening until Paige suggested they should get some sleep, tomorrow was going to be a long day.

Angel couldn't sleep. He lay in a sleeping bag on the sofa, thinking of all that had happened and trying to imagine what was to come. He thought of Paige too. Angel was excited at the prospect of them spending time together. She gave him butterflies. It was a long time since a woman had had that effect on him. But it wasn't long until thoughts of his mother returned. A cloud of sadness broke over him and he cried quietly into his pillow.

CHAPTER 22

"Hi, Julia," smiled Delores. "How are you?"

She was sitting in a booth in one of the capital's best restaurants when the former White House intern arrived.

"I'm doing great thanks. I was surprised to get your call, though."

"I know, I feel bad for not calling sooner. It's not that I didn't want to see you. It's just that I've been so busy."

"Hi, I'm Jerome, I'll be serving you today." A young man interrupted them.

"I'll have a Waldorf salad, but you probably need a couple of minutes," said Delores.

"No, I'll have the same."

"And to drink?" asked the waiter.

"Two glasses of champagne," said Delores.

"Wow," Julia said after the waiter left. "Are we celebrating?"

"Yes, I hear you've got a great new job."

"I did have. The President himself recommended me for it. I wouldn't have got it otherwise, but I got laid off a few months ago."

"Oh my, I'm sorry to hear that. Well, let's enjoy the champagne. After all, you don't have to go back to the office this afternoon."

They both laughed.

"I do have an appointment to see a realtor later. I bought a great apartment, but I'm behind on the mortgage payments, and need to get it sold before the bank forecloses on me. Anyway, enough of my problems, it's so great to see you again, Delores. You know I really appreciated your support last summer when I was working at the White House. Though I felt bad that I told you about me and the President. You seemed kind of upset with me for mentioning it."

"To be honest, I guess I was. I thought the worst thing for our country back then would be a long drawn out scandal which would have brought the government to a halt when so many important things needed addressing."

Delores stopped talking, Jerome had arrived with the champagne.

"Cheers," said Delores, "Here's to better days."

They clinked their glasses together.

"You said back then. Have things changed?" asked Julia.

"Yes, I think they have. It concerns me that we have an election coming soon, and the electorate doesn't know the kind of man he is. In a democratic society like ours, the voters are entitled to know the truth, the whole truth about those they're going to be asked to vote for this fall."

Jerome served their salads and their conversation halted temporarily again.

"So?" prompted Julia when he had gone.

"I suppose what I'm saying is that if you wanted to go public, then in my opinion, it would be the right thing to do. You'd be doing a service to our democracy. You would make a whole bunch of money too. Exclusive story rights, talk shows, all that stuff."

"Well, I can't deny the money would come in very handy right now."

" But I don't want you to be under any illusions, Julia. It would be a demanding time for you. For a while you would be under media scrutiny twenty-four seven. Those with vested interests, and there are plenty of them, believe me, would be out to make you look bad. You have to ask yourself if you really want that kind of pressure."

"I understand what you're saying. I've often thought about it, and what I'd have to go through but I want to do it. I wanted to do it before but I never knew how. Could you help me?"

"I shouldn't get involved. I'm sure Ted and his team would only use that against you."

"Oh..." Julia looked down at her food to hide her disappointment.

"If I was seen to be helping you, they would portray it as an act of revenge for not putting me on the ticket. If you've followed the news recently, you'll know he's chosen Linda Hernandez instead of me. My involvement would take the focus away from the truth and the story that needs to be told. But here's what I can do, I can put you in touch with a journalist I know who would get your story out there for you. She's the best in her class."

"You would do that for me?"

"Sure. I'll call her this afternoon."

Delores smiled. This had turned out to be easier than she'd expected.

At her desk later that afternoon, Delores thought how Julia would find it incredibly hard to find a job once the matter became public. Employers would shun hiring someone of such notoriety. Some may have fretted whether they were doing the right thing but not Delores. She'd convinced herself long ago that nothing mattered more than achieving her goal. Picking up the phone, she called the journalist.

CHAPTER 23

When their small ski plane lifted off the ground, a buzz shot through Angel. He had never flown before. Instantly, he knew this was an experience he wanted to repeat. It was noisy and thrilling, unlike the clinical atmosphere of a jet airliner which is most people's experience of flying. Seated up front, he was riding shotgun with the pilot, a middle aged woman with big blond hair by the name of Maisie. Paige was sitting behind him. There were only four seats and a space for luggage at the rear. They wore headphones to be able to hear the pilot and lessen the noise of the propeller at the front.

"Wow!" exclaimed Angel when he momentarily left his stomach a hundred feet above him when they hit some turbulence.

"Yeah, it sure is something eh?" said Maisie. "I've been doing this for ten years now but never get tired of it. I fly float planes in summer and ski planes in winter. Every morning I come to work with a big old grin on my face."

Below, the signs of human habitation became ever less frequent until they disappeared altogether to be replaced by an interminable winter ocean of forest and frozen lakes.

They landed halfway to refuel and then continued their journey north. Although the days were lengthening, dusk was approaching when they finally descended toward their destination and circled above a frozen lake on which a rudimentary ice runway had been prepared. On landing, the plane hit the ground hard and bounced into the air again before there was another thump as they hit the ice a second and final time.

Maisie taxied the plane to the edge of the lake by which stood a small First Nation settlement. When they jumped down from the plane, the cold nearly took their breath away. Saskatoon had been freezing. The temperature up here was significantly lower still. A few of the local First Nation men stood expressionless watching their arrival.

"Hi there," said Angel. "I was hoping you could help us. We've come to see Mingan. He said to get here and one of you guys would be able to get us over to his place."

"I can do that," said one of them stepping forward. "It's about thirty kilometers. It'll cost five hundred dollars."

"Five hundred!"

"That's fine," said Paige.

"I'll take you in the morning, it's already too late today. You can sleep at my place tonight. Follow me. The name's Joe."

They trudged after him through the snow and up a short street of prefab homes, stopping to watch the plane take off and turn south. Joe's wife stood at the door of the last dwelling and greeted them with a warm smile.

"Come on in, you must be tired and hungry." She sat them down in the kitchen area and ladled some stew from a pot on the stove. "Caribou, it's the best."

They hadn't eaten all day and practically inhaled it. Joe and his wife quizzed them about their trip. Angel explained how he'd met Mingan and his family last summer and was taking up the open invitation to visit.

"Why now?"

"Well, I don't get to see much snow in Phoenix so I thought winter would be a good time. I heard mosquitoes are a problem up here in the summer."

"They can be. You two been together long?"

"Us? Oh no, we're just good friends," replied Paige.

That night, they both slept on the floor in sleeping bags their hosts had provided. Joe woke them early.

"We need to get going. I gotta be back as soon as I can."

His wife gave them some breakfast and then they went outside to join Joe, who was securing their backpacks to a trailer attached to a snowmobile.

"Paige, you can get on the back of mine, and, Angel, you can take the other one."

Angel looked quizzically at the machine.

"Guess you've never driven one of these before, eh?"

"No sir, can't say I have. There ain't much call for them in Arizona."

"It's not difficult, you just need to lean into turns and keep your speed up. Going too slow is worse than going too fast. Here's how you adjust the throttle. Watch what I do and you'll be okay."

And with that peremptory instruction, Joe sat astride his snowmobile with Paige seated behind him and they were off, pulling the luggage trailer with them.

Angel followed, it didn't seem so difficult after all. At least that's what he thought initially. But once they left the marked trail, his assessment changed abruptly as he got stuck for the first of several times in deeper snow or turned the machine on its side, leaving him prostrate on the ground when he failed to take the corners properly. These experiences caused him to go more slowly, which only made matters worse.

Angel's ignominy was complete when Joe asked Paige how she would feel about driving and Angel had to get on the back of Joe's snowmobile. Paige took to it like a natural. When they stopped for a break, he asked Joe for another chance. Angel needed to redeem his masculinity. This time he put more aggression into it and it worked.

He began to relax and enjoy the ride. It was fun as well as incredibly beautiful. They were speeding through a pristine wilderness of pure white, the snow sparkling like millions of diamonds in the sharp sunlight.

After a couple of hours, they reached the shoreside cabin of Abbie and Mingan. Hearing their approach they had come outside, standing with their son, Wematin, to watch the arrival of three strangers with a look of bemusement. The travelers' faces were hidden behind their face masks which they were wearing to keep out the biting cold. Joe removed his first.

"Hey Joe, I wasn't expecting to see you this

side of June. Who've you got with you? Oh my, it can't be, can it?"

"Hi man, good to see you," said Angel hugging Mingan and then Abbie. "Well, you said to visit anytime so I have."

"We sure did, and it's great to have you both," said Abbie.

"This is Paige."

"Hi Paige, great to meet you."

"I have to shoot straight back," said Joe as soon as he'd unloaded their luggage.

"Thanks for bringing us here," said Angel.

"When do you want to be brought back?"

"We're not really sure..."

"Don't worry about that, I'll bring them back on the sled," interjected Mingan. "Let's go inside, you must be cold after your ride."

The cabin was cozy, an oasis of warmth from the bewitching but harsh world outside. Abbie poured them some coffee.

"We're real pleased you finally made it up and with your..." Mingan hesitated, searching for the right word.

"I'm not his girlfriend, we're just friends," said Paige.

"What do you want to do while you're here? The cold kinda limits our options."

"Unfortunately, we haven't come for a vacation. There's something bad, really bad going on."

Angel told them about his mother's murder and the pipeline.

"That's truly shocking. What do you plan to do exactly?" asked Mingan.

"I thought we could go check out what's going on. Get some evidence so people will believe me. Maybe it'll create enough of an upset to bring the whole thing to a halt."

"Do you realize how big this country is?"

"Kinda, but we can't just let them get away with it."

"Well, I guess we can go look but it's gonna be a long hard journey to get up to Athabasca. I agree what they've done and what they have planned is awful, and I certainly want to do anything I can to stop them. We'll get going at first light tomorrow."

That night they ate more caribou as they would on many more occasions in the coming days. They relished the heat and comforting light cast by the fire. The cabin felt safe, a world away from what they were about to embark upon. Though none of them said so, they each couldn't get out of their mind that this evening would soon pass and a cold dawn of travel into the unknown would arrive. An unknown which would show them no mercy. One mistake out there could mean death.

Abbie laid out animal furs for Paige and Angel to sleep on. When they awoke, she was already up making breakfast; more caribou. She encouraged them to eat heartily. There might not be much hot food in the coming days, she told them. Mingan was outside, and they could tell from the excited barking of the dogs that he was getting a sled ready.

Angel ventured out into the early morning. It was as if he had climbed into a freezer and shut the door on himself. Mingan was preparing two sleds.

"I'll take one with our kit and supplies, and you and Paige can take the other."

"But I've never mushed before."

"Until yesterday, you'd never snowmobiled either. It's not difficult and you'll be following me."

Mingan had already loaded his sled and began positioning the dogs, six on each sled.

"The two closest to the sled are the wheel

dogs. In bigger teams you then have the team dogs, but we don't have enough. I need to leave some with Abbie, so next I'll put the swing dogs to get us round the turns, and then the lead dogs to take the lead and set the pace. There's quite an art to it. You've got to know the temperament of each dog to position them right or you'll be in all kinds of trouble."

"They're beautiful."

"That they sure are, eh? They're incredible animals," said Mingan, bending down to stroke one. "They make it possible for us to live here. For thousands of years they've been our friends and helpers."

Paige and Abbie joined them.

"Okay," shouted Mingan above the cacophony of barking. The excited huskies were yearning to be underway. "We're about ready now. Paige, why don't you make yourself comfortable on the sled. You can try mushing in a while."

"I hope Angel's better at mushing than snowmobiling," she teased.

Mingan went over to Abbie who looked close to tears and gave her a hug.

"Don't you worry, we'll be back before you know it."

Picking up Wematin, who'd also emerged from the cabin, Mingan swung him around in the air several times to squeals of delight and demands for more.

"You all take care now," said Abbie forcing a smile. "Don't go doing anything stupid."

Handing Wematin to her, Mingan stepped onto the wooden bar across the bottom of the back of his sled. Paige snuggled under a fur on the second sled and Angel stood behind her.

"Right, Angel," said Mingan. "Shout 'Hike' to get them moving and 'Whoa' to stop. And 'Easy' to slow down. They should follow what I do anyways."

Angel's muscles tensed, he was hoping he wouldn't embarrass himself again in front of Paige like he had yesterday. Natural instincts urged him to impress her that he had command of these beasts, that he could provide for her and be a suitable mate. To his relief, he found it easier than snowmobiling and they moved off smoothly behind Mingan.

The snow was dry and powdery, the air pure and bracing. Their eyelashes frosted over and the cold stung the inside of their nostrils, yet it was pure joy to be out here. It was another glorious sunny day. They were enveloped by the quietest quiet. The natural world still slept, waiting for spring to wake it from winter's spell. The silence was almost loud.

The huskies loved to pull and run, their tongues hanging out; they were born to do this. They traveled fast across the lake and then through forest all bedecked in snow. To Angel, it felt even more exhilarating than snowmobiling had, a closer connection with nature. Only man, animal, and the great outdoors. He half ran, half rode as he dodged low hanging branches, a look of sheer delight written large across his face.

His smile was briefly but abruptly removed when he took a corner and came off. The dogs carried on regardless with Paige on the sled until they caught up with Mingan. He laughed as Angel, covered in snow from top to bottom, came toward them.

"I probably forgot to mention that you need to hit the brake before a turn. If you don't brake until you reach the turn, you'll lose control and come off."

"No, you didn't mention that," said Angel pointedly.

They traveled for several hours with only a few short stops until Mingan called a final halt for the day.

"We'll camp here tonight. First, I need to feed the dogs."

He threw them some meat and then built a fire, telling Angel and Paige to warm themselves next to it. From the sled, he unloaded a tent made from caribou hide.

Like the huskies, the caribou was an essential component of man's survival in this land. Caribou hair has incredible insulating properties, evolved from living countless millennia in their Arctic environment. Clothing made from it also has the advantage of being lightweight, water repellant, and durable. Mingan wore a parka made from caribou, the fur being worn on the inside and a hood with a wolverine ruff around it creating a pool of warmth for his face. His pants too were made from caribou as were his boots and mittens. He never complained of the cold. Angel and Paige with the latest hi-tech branded garments would feel it more than Mingan ever did.

Mingan worked like a demon. That first evening Angel and Paige could only watch, their offers of help declined, wanting to assist but not knowing what they should do. By the second day, having witnessed the routine they didn't ask if they could help, they just took their cue from what Mingan was doing and performed the next task.

He finished erecting the tent in which he placed a lamp that burned caribou fat to provide both warmth and light. Mingan then placed rocks in the fire outside which later would be used to provide added warmth inside the tent. It turned out to be remarkably toasty inside despite the sub zero conditions outside.

He melted some snow in a pot hung above the fire to provide water and made them a hot drink containing pine needles which he explained are packed with vitamin C. Mingan then made holes in the ice on the lake next to where they were camped and lowered bait on a line. Next, he shoved branches taken from a nearby spruce tree into the holes, and covered them with snow for insulation to stop the holes freezing over again. The following morning, there was a good size fish on the line in each hole, supplementing the supplies they'd brought with them.

The days blurred into one as they settled into a routine of breaking camp, traveling all day, and then making camp again. Their daily diet of caribou and fish became distinctly unappetizing, and the thrill of the first day's mushing morphed into an endurance test. The landscape remained unaltered; forest, frozen rivers, and lakes, seemingly without end. The weather had changed to low gray clouds, eliminating color and depth from the landscape.

They mushed in a trance-like state,

barely communicating with each other. They were becoming weary. By contrast, the dogs' boundless energy was showing no sign of diminishing.

After several days as the light was fading, the landscape opened up onto a lake incomparably larger than any they had seen thus far. Mingan called a halt and they surveyed the great flat expanse before them.

"Lake Athabasca," he announced with satisfaction.

At nearly two hundred miles long and fifty miles wide it was big, although much smaller than the considerably larger Great Bear and Great Slave Lakes from where the pipeline would begin. Angel wondered in how so vast a space they could ever locate where the pipeline was.

"We are toward the eastern edge," explained Mingan. "My guess would be the pipeline will be over this way. We'll explore tomorrow."

They found nothing that day. The next as they rounded a bluff near the lake shore, Mingan brought them to a sudden halt. Not much more than a mile away, they could see construction and large machines.

"It looks like we've found it," said Mingan. "Let's retreat and make camp far enough away that the dogs won't be heard. We'll go over there after nightfall.

When darkness fell Paige and Angel readied themselves. Paige produced night vision goggles with built-in photo capability. Mingan made no move to get ready.

"Guys, are you okay to go without me? I want to stay here and watch the dogs."

"Sure," replied Angel.

"If you're not back in a couple of hours, I'll come looking for you."

"Make it three."

He and Paige trudged off wearing snowshoes Mingan had brought, another invention of the indigenous people of North America which was perfectly adapted to their environment. They spread out their weight and stopped them sinking into the snow. Had they tried walking that far without snowshoes, it would have taken much longer and been much more tiring.

They'd already used them before around camp with some instruction from Mingan. They had learned how to lift the shoes slightly and slide the inner edge of the shoes over each other to make walking easier, how to dig in the toes in the snow when climbing, and to use exaggerated steps running down hill.

Angel felt his pulse quicken, not from

exertion but from a mixture of the excitement of finally being here at their goal and the fear of being discovered. Although the snow muffled the sound of their movement, he worried they might run into someone.

Bright lights illuminated the site and work was still continuing. Clearly they were working around the clock to get it built as quickly as possible. Angel and Paige kept to the edge of the forest. With their night vision goggles they could see perfectly and zoom in until they could even identify individual workers. Angel started the record on his goggles, panning the site. What appeared to be four pipelines, two side by side and two above those, which were only visible when zoomed in close, stretched southward from the lake shore where a large building without windows was under construction. Several portable buildings to house the workers were located nearby.

"What do you think they're building?" he asked.

"A pumping station to get the water out of the lake and moving down the pipelines. We should come back tomorrow and get some daylight shots."

After half an hour of watching and filming the scene, they returned to their camp. The following morning, they were back getting further video. This time, they also noticed a military vehicle and US army insignia on the clothes of the personnel.

By noon, they were back at camp with all the evidence they needed. Mingan had already loaded everything back onto the sleds in preparation for their long journey south. After several days of gray clouds, sunshine had returned. It was almost April now. The days were lengthening fast and the temperature was rising noticeably. The change in weather matched the change in their mood. In high spirits, they set off on their journey home. They'd succeeded in getting what they had traveled across uncompromising wilderness for many days to find.

CHAPTER 24

That evening, Ethan sat on his bed in his apartment in Washington DC, his cell phone in his hand.

A week ago, the guy who had accosted him at the Royalton in New York and threatened to turn his life upside down, found him again while he sat drinking a beer and watching a football game in a bar after work.

"Do you mind if I join you?" asked the unwelcome visitor rhetorically. "What news have you got for me?"

"I'm still working on it."

"Working on it? Well, you've sure been working on her. I've heard you banging her but never once asking her what you're supposed to, why is that?"

"What?" Ethan snarled.

"Your place is bugged, stupid. Look, the guys paying me are getting tired of waiting. You bring me some news in the next week, or we'll release your secret. Enjoy the game."

After he left, Ethan sat nursing his beer for comfort. He thought of the promise which he'd given Ann, he couldn't betray her but if he didn't he was finished. Everything he had worked so hard for would be destroyed... but wait a minute; I don't have to just be the victim here, he told himself. I could do something about it, meet fire with fire.

The next day, Ethan hired his own private detective to find out who the man was and who he was working for. It had cost him a lot, but it was worth it. Ethan had developed strong feelings for Ann. It was strange, she was old enough to be his mother, yet he found her more satisfying both sexually and intellectually than the women his own age that he'd dated. He wasn't going to let her down.

The guy he hired had reported back yesterday. The man went by the name of Marty Eckstein and was working for the Republicans, exactly as Ethan thought might be the case.

Ethan dialed his number.

"It's Ethan."

"About time. You better have some news for me."

"I do."

"Good, well let's hear it then."

"I'm not going to give you the information you want. In fact, I'll be going to the newspapers if you and your Republican paymasters don't back off."

There was a short silence on the other end of the line, Eckstein had been blindsided.

"I sure as hell wouldn't do that if I were you. You don't understand, you're in way over your head. You can't-"

Ethan hung up. He figured he'd done enough to get rid of them. Although he didn't want the scrutiny and intrusion of a media feeding frenzy, he was confident the Republicans wouldn't want their dirty tricks uncovered either. He lay down and closed his eyes, satisfied he had outsmarted them.

Ann arrived about ten. She wanted to surprise him. Hidden under her coat, she wore a costume she felt sure would please him. She was dressed as a waitress from the Oktoberfest, but unlike the fraus of Munich's bierkellers, who carried twenty steins of beer at a time engulfed in their large arms and pressed against their ample bosom, her outfit was a skimpy one, a plunging neckline and a skirt which would be indecent in public, beneath which she wore nothing.

"Guten abend mein Herr," she called out in jest. "Mein name is Heidi and I'm here to service your every desire."

There was no reply.

"Hey, Ethan it's me."

Ann opened the door to his bedroom. He lay there asleep on the bed. She went back into the living area and took off her coat, arranging her outfit to best effect and smiled at herself in the mirror on the wall. Tonight would be one to enjoy, one to remember, a night of pure hedonism.

Ann grabbed a beer from the fridge for him, opened it, took a swig of it herself, and returned to the bedroom to wake him. She couldn't wait to see his face when he woke up, a beer and a fantasy come true. That should make him happy. He'd seemed preoccupied of late, stressed and agitated. He was probably working too hard. He needed a little fun, just like she did.

"Wake up, hon, and see what you're missing."

Ethan didn't stir. She ran her hand down his cheek to wake him but immediately drew back in horror. He was cold, stone cold. Then she saw it. A bullet wound on the side of his neck farthest from her. Blood on his pillow case and the sheets underneath. Ann swayed. Her legs crumbled under her and she fell to her knees.

Leaning forward, she placed her hands on the floor and vomited. As she did so, she felt something solid under her left hand. A gun. She got up quickly. Who could have done this and why? What if the killer was still in the apartment?

Hurrying from the bedroom, she picked up her coat and raced out. She ran across the street to her car and drove back to her house. Going inside, she closed the front door, bolted it, and sank to the floor sobbing uncontrollably for several minutes.

Regaining her self control slightly, Ann called 911 on a government issued phone they wouldn't be able to trace.

"There's been a murder." She broke down again.

"Where ma'am?"

There was no response.

"Ma'am, are you still there? I need an address."

Ann gave the address and hung up.

She remained on the floor until almost dawn, still reeling from the shock. Ethan, her lover, her wonderful lover, the man who had made her feel a woman again, was dead.

Murdered.

Finally, she got up and walked unsteadily to the kitchen. Making herself a strong coffee, she retreated to her bedroom. Ann rang her assistant and told her to cancel all her appointments for the day, a bad case of food poisoning, and she wouldn't be taking any calls either.

CHAPTER 25

That very same night, Angel and Paige were rewarded with the Northern Lights. Sitting by the campfire, they were spellbound. Nature put on a display more spectacular than anything either of them had ever witnessed. It was as if a hologram of shimmering greens, whites, and purples had been projected onto the big screen of the dark sky, reaching toward earth from the heavens. Ethereal curtains of light hundreds of miles high danced above them, a cosmic light show provided by the sun whose solar particles mixing with earth's atmosphere created these photons of light.

For the Cree, the Aurora Borealis ties in with their belief in the circle of life in which the dead are not completely separated from their loved ones and will look for ways to communicate with them.

They moved away from the campfire to get a better view. For a long time they stood in silence, transfixed by the sheer wonder of it, their faces alight with joy and oblivious to the cold night.

Paige grabbed Angel's hand and smiled at him. He smiled back and she squeezed his hand tightly. The Aurora provided the perfect setting to acknowledge the feelings he believed were developing between them. What more romantic a setting could there be, out here miles from anywhere on a crisp winter's night experiencing the awe and wonder of the universe.

It reminded Angel of how insignificant man and all his technology really was. Nature demanded balance and if man disturbed that, nature would restore it.

"Time to get some sleep," said Paige. She ran her hand gently down the scar on his cheek and kissed him briefly on the mouth before walking back to the tent where Mingan was already snoring.

Next day, they set off with renewed vigor, still on a high from nature's pyrotechnics though tired from staying up so late to watch them. Around noon, while they crossed one of the tens of frozen lakes on their journey home, Paige who was sitting on one of the sleds, experienced that uncomfortable feeling of being watched. She looked around but could see no one. Stop being paranoid, she scolded herself. No one had seen them near the pumping station, no one knew about them. How could there possibly be anyone else out here in the middle of nowhere?

Then only a few moments later, she noticed a definite movement coming from the forest on the east side of the lake, to their left. Who was following them? While she stared at the spot, a wolf emerged and then more.

"Hey, look! Over there."

About twenty wolves had appeared and were running parallel to them along the edge of the lake. The wolves soon noticed that they too were being watched and came to a halt, looking longingly at the humans and their dogs. They had thick winter fur and the long legs distinctive of their species that were so useful to navigate deep snow. They were desperate for food, thin and hungry after a long winter. Each of them salivated, they hadn't seen so much meat since last summer. The wolves had the same almond shape eyes as the huskies, yet despite their malnourishment were almost twice their size with jaws considerably stronger than those of their tamed cousins.

"I was wondering when we would run into a pack," said Mingan casually, stopping his sled. Angel and Paige came to a halt beside him. "No need to worry, they won't bother us."

He took his rifle from the sled, aimed and fired. One fell to the ground, dead. The others retreated quickly into the forest.

"Are they gone?" asked Paige.

"Probably. I expect they're off looking for an easier target."

Of course it made perfect sense that there would be wolves out here, even if it still came as a surprise to Angel and Paige. It was something to which they hadn't given a moment's thought, until now. They had seen little wildlife since leaving the cabin; some woodland caribou, a glimpse of a lynx. The bears and many other mammals were hibernating still, and birds had flown south for the winter. But the wolf was always active whatever the season, constantly on the move, hunting for his next meal. A creature which had a mythical status deeply embedded in the human psyche, feared by man since the earliest of times. A dark shadow on the periphery of man's consciousness, and an uncomfortable reminder of his place in the food chain in a world stripped back to the basics.

They made good progress that day. Mingan called a halt only when it was too dark to continue. They made camp in a clearing in the woods and sat around the fire, entranced by watching the flames dance in the dark. The scene was timeless. For thousands of years, the native peoples who lived in this region had done the same.

Warm and full of caribou meat, they were

all looking forward to a good night's rest. A mournful howl abruptly interrupted their evening, followed closely by more. They said nothing but they understood. The wolves hadn't gone away. The huskies moved in closer to the fire, unnerved by the sound. They sensed malevolent spirits in the night air.

"I'll sit out here tonight and keep watch," said Mingan.

"I'll stay with you," volunteered Angel. "Why don't you go get some sleep, Paige."

"I don't think I could."

Mingan built up the fire and fetched his rifle. He sat holding it, waiting. Waiting for any attempt by the wolves to attack.

The howls ended. There was complete silence apart from the crackle of the fire. They began to believe the wolves had indeed moved on. But then they saw them: pairs of eyes, between the trunks of the pine trees, eyes which were watching them intently. Mingan stood up and shouted at them. They didn't move. He fired a shot with his rifle. The wolves disappeared. All they could see now was darkness between the trees, but they knew the wolves were there, just out of sight and biding their time.

An hour passed, maybe longer. All three of them fought to stay awake, they wanted nothing more than to close their eyes and sleep. Sleep, if only for a few moments...

The yelps of the dogs woke them all. The humans jumped up, very much awake. They were too late, one of the huskies was already being dragged off into the forest. Mingan grabbed his rifle and fired into the black space between the trees. It was a futile gesture. He fired again and again at the eyes of death in the forest staring at them but they simply melted away.

It seemed like an eternity until dawn. When morning finally came, they quickly broke camp to continue their journey. There was no lingering over a hot drink. They drank some water and fed the dogs. Yesterday's elation of mission accomplished had given way to a deep angst. On edge as though they'd overdosed on caffeine, they knew they must get back to the safety of the cabin as soon as they could, but it was still two or three days away.

Through the trees they could see that the wolves were accompanying them on their journey. These animals had tasted blood and wanted more. One dog between twenty wolves was but a morsel. They still burned with hunger, it had been so long since they had eaten a decent meal. For creatures in this unforgiving land, survival was a constant battle. They had found a rarity, a source of bounty. Wolves are patient and relentless hunters, waiting for that one moment of vulnerability. Then they would pounce and sink their hugely powerful canines into warm flesh and get the nourishment needed to sustain them until the bitter harvest of winter would finally release its grip.

Mingan drove his party toward a frozen river. He wanted to be in more open country. Weaving through the trees exposed them to easier attack. The wolves followed them at a safe distance. They understood he could kill with his stick that made a noise. The huskies ran faster than usual. They had seen what had happened to one of their own. Each now was running with extra effort, sensing that his life depended on it.

Around midday, they reached yet another frozen lake and began to cross it. They were a few hundred feet out when suddenly the ice under Mingan's sled began to break. Angel managed to halt his team of dogs before reaching the spot. He and Paige looked on in horror while the heavy sled went through the ice and began sinking inexorably into the deep water beneath.

The huskies were straining to go forward as they felt the sled behind them dive at a steep angle, pulling them with it. Despite their frantic efforts, they couldn't combat the backward and downward force. The huskies tied to each other and the sled had no chance. They disappeared from view beneath the surface of the lake, uttering a haunting, whimpering sound. Down with them went the night vision goggles, containing the photographic evidence which Angel and Paige had risked their lives for.

Mingan was in the water too, desperately trying to escape. Repeatedly he grabbed at the ice to pull himself out, but each time it broke off into pieces as he did so, leaving him floundering in the dark, opaque water and fast losing the energy needed to keep his head above the surface. It wouldn't be long until this watery grave claimed him as a victim. Angel hurried toward him.

"You need to get down, approach on your stomach to spread your weight," spluttered Mingan.

Angel did so and made his way forward in an ungainly manner, like a seal on land. He reached out for Mingan's hands and pulled, but he didn't have the strength to haul him out. Mingan was disappearing beneath the surface for ever longer periods. Angel and Paige would die as well. Without Mingan, they would perish. They didn't know the way back.

Paige too had slithered over the ice. She got up onto her knees and took hold of Angel's feet and pulled with all her might. The ice beneath them made ominous cracking sounds, however this extra force was enough to get Mingan out of the water. Each taking one of his arms, Angel and Paige wiggled backward, still lying on the ice, and pulled Mingan as if he were a carcass to where the ice was firmer. He lay immobile, panting with exhaustion, and shivering.

"We need to get off the ice," said Paige.

They manhandled Mingan onto the remaining sled and headed back toward the shore. The wolves not knowing that Mingan's rifle was now many feet under the ice, withdrew into the forest by the lake shore as they approached.

"Take his wet clothes off and strip to your underwear," commanded Paige. "We need to get under the caribou skins with him and hug him to warm him up with our body heat."

Gradually, the warmth from them both brought him back from the edge of hypothermia. They rummaged through what they had left to find some dry clothes for him.

The seriousness of their predicament bore down on them. They were extremely vulnerable. Most of their supplies were gone, and they only had one sled and six dogs between them. About one hundred feet away, the wolves stared at them.

"We need to get going again as soon as possible," insisted Mingan still shivering.

They went around the shore of the lake this time. Taking it in turns, they half ran and half walked alongside using snowshoes. The remaining dogs could not pull all three of them. Out on the lake the wolves shadowed them, always watching, always waiting, ready to take that opportunity should it present itself as surely it now must. They perceived the change in the balance of power. Their infinite patience and determination were beginning to pay off. In the air, they could smell the humans' fear.

Once past the lake, it was but a short distance to the next and the humans reached the far side of that other lake before the light began to fade. Mingan called a halt.

"We'll rest here tonight and follow the frozen river in the morning. With luck, we'll make it back tomorrow."

This news raised their spirits. Only one last night to endure, less than twenty-four hours until they would be free from this living nightmare.

Their tent had been lost, not that it really mattered anymore. They needed to guard the dogs, and none of them would have wanted to sleep in a tent away from the fire. With fire they could keep the wolves at bay. They broke off low hanging branches from trees which were near to them and built up a roaring fire as quickly as they could. It would soon be dark, and out here night was no friend to them.

Incredibly tired after today's challenges and from getting virtually no sleep in over twenty-four hours, their limbs felt clumsy and heavy.

"We'll take turns to keep watch. I'll go first," said Mingan.

Already, out beyond the glow of the fire, they could see those eyes; many pairs, silently studying them. One wolf approached, and then came even nearer to test them. He watched Mingan's every move, waiting for him to produce the stick that killed. He didn't. Emboldened, the wolf came closer to the fire and others followed. The dogs huddled in around the humans. Mingan picked up a stick from the edge of the fire, brandishing it angrily. Advancing toward the wolf, he threw the stick at him. The wolf yelped as it hit him, burning his flesh. He retreated quickly as did the other wolves.

The commotion awoke Angel and Paige who had been dozing. Throughout the night, the wolves tried, and tried again, snarling and determined. Each time the humans drove them back, throwing or waving burning branches at them until their supply was almost exhausted. Sleep was impossible. They only got a moment now and then when their eyes would no longer stay open and they lost the fight to stay awake.

How they yearned to close their eyes and rest, if only for a little while.

Dawn, when it arrived, was foggy and without that sense of hope a new day brings. Snow began falling and visibility soon became extremely limited. They hitched the remaining huskies to the sled and set off down the frozen river which drained the lake. Before long a swirling blizzard set in. Being unable to see more than a few yards in any direction was disturbing, and raised their anxiety level to a new height. They knew the wolves were tracking them, but whether they were behind, to the side, or in front, they couldn't tell. They continued for some time, not daring to stop, not even for a moment.

Then out of the gray they came, running sideways at them toward the dogs. Their teeth bared and lips pulled back as they growled. They lunged at the huskies. Operating as one efficient killing machine, three wolves targeted each dog. They pulled them over and bit into them.

Paige screamed with fright as the sled went over on its side with her on it. Mingan and Angel quickly pulled her up. Hurriedly, they withdrew into the forest. There was nothing they could do to save the poor huskies. They had to try and save themselves. They were completely defenseless now.

Tears stung Mingan's eyes. He loved those animals and the ones who died yesterday. They had served him faithfully, always eager and reliable, the best friend a man out here could have. But in this place there was no time for grief. The laws of nature didn't recognize it. Emotion had no relevance to survival. Death was part of life. Their deaths saved the wolves from starvation and the circle of life would keep on turning.

"What do we do now?" asked Paige, the fear quite apparent in her voice.

"We carry on. They'll be a while devouring their kill. It gives us the chance to get away."

The dogs should satisfy the wolves' immediate hunger. But Mingan was concerned they would still come after them. He knew they offered another easy kill, a rare opportunity which the wolves wouldn't want to waste. The three of them stumbled off through the deepening snow as quickly as they could manage. No one talked, all their focus was on moving forward, getting back. Their instinct to survive drove them on. They fought the images tormenting their minds. Images of wolves leaping out of the blizzard and taking them down.

All day they pushed on through the snow, their pace becoming ever slower as the cold and lack of food and drink took their toll. When evening approached, the storm abated. They looked anxiously behind. All they could see was forest heavy with snow, branches bent low with the weight of it. Could it be the wolves were satiated? They had no way of knowing so they continued to press on, propelled by fear. The wolves could easily follow the tracks they had left in the snow and travel fifty miles in a day. They would have no difficulty catching up. Daylight would soon be gone and the humans would be out here in total darkness. They had nothing to light a fire with, and nothing to ward off attack. If the wolves came after them, it would all be over.

Then they saw it. The blessed sight of the lake they had started out from, and on the far side of it smoke rising into the air from the cabin. Despite their extreme fatigue, they quickened their pace, stumbling like drunkards toward their goal, falling frequently in the snow, but smiling at each other in their relief. The stress which had been weighing down on them with such pressure for so many hours had finally lifted.

Abbie noticed them coming and emerged from the cabin. She knew something terrible must have happened because they were alone. She ran toward them and into Mingan's waiting arms.

"Thank God you're back safe. Let's get you all inside, you must be so cold."

Wematin had come out now too. He ran up to his father and embraced his legs. Mingan picked him up and held him tightly and kissed his head, so relieved that he had made it back to his family. They gratefully followed Abbie into the cabin.

Abbie made them a hot drink and began preparing food while they told her about their ordeal. With her back to them she blinked back tears, upset at the loss of their dogs and how close Mingan had come to never making it home.

While they devoured their first meal in over a day, Angel explained what they'd seen up at Lake Athabasca.

"What will you do now?" asked Abbie, concern in her voice. She was fearful for her family as to what the consequences of Mingan's involvement might be.

"I want to go back to the States, back to Phoenix where they murdered my mom and confront the Governor. Get it out there on the networks. Once folks know exactly what is going on up here, there'll be a fricking earthquake. The publicity should end all this madness, put a stop to the pipeline. But don't you worry, Abbie. No one will ever know that you and Mingan were involved."

That night they slept the sleep of the saved, warmed by the fire and cocooned in the protection of the cabin.

CHAPTER 26

The following morning in DC, the President was chairing the weekly meeting to review progress on the pipelines with Chip, Ann, Kim and various aides in attendance.

“Okay folks, let’s get started. Give me an update on progress since last week.”

“Mr. President, sir,” began an aide from the Pentagon. “The pumping station at Athabasca is due to be completed in a month, ahead of schedule. Pipeline construction is...well, it’s going slower than anticipated.”

“How much slower?”

“Er…several weeks off the timeline, sir.”

“That’s just not acceptable. Why haven’t I been told this before?”

“We only got the news ourselves two days ago.”

“It seems to me you need to improve your monitoring and communication strategies pretty damn fast then," retorted Ted tersely, his anger clear for all to hear.

"We need more resources," said Chip.

"Well get them!"

"I can do that but it will mean relocating troops from other duties where they are sorely needed. We've already diverted many thousands to the project, and left important areas elsewhere exposed with a shortage of manpower."

"Look, like I've said many times already, nothing, I repeat nothing, is more important than this task. Failure to get that water flowing on time is the biggest threat to our nation's security, period. I want you to assign as many personnel as are needed, and cancel all leave until we're not only back on track but well ahead of schedule. Have I made myself clear?"

"Yes sir, crystal clear."

"Ann, how are the Canadians holding up?"

She didn't answer. Slouched in her chair, she was staring into space.

"Ann!" His voice was much louder this time, annoyed by her inattention at this crucial time. She sat up sharply, embarrassment coloring her cheeks.

"I'm sorry. I didn't quite catch that, Mr. President."

“I said we will increase troop numbers to get back on schedule. How are things going with the Canadians?”

“Oh...good, generally good. But if any surge in boots on the ground means more of our boys in Canada, they won’t be happy about that. I can ask them but I anticipate they would refuse any such request.”

“Then we won’t tell them. We’ll send the troops in covertly. If word gets out about the pipeline before it’s finished, the more of our troops we have up there protecting it the better in case those Canadians turn difficult on us. We need to wrap this up. When we meet next week I expect confirmation, Chip, that you have done what is needed to get us back on schedule. Ann, could you stay a minute?”

“Ann,” he began after the others had departed, “Are you sure you’re feeling okay? You don’t seem yourself at all.”

“Me? Oh I’m fine. Just fine, really.”

“If I know you, you’ve been working too hard. Take it easy for a couple of days. Rest up a little.”

“Maybe. Will that be all, sir?”

“Yes, but if something’s bothering you, you know you can talk to me.”

"Thanks, I appreciate that."

She got up and walked away from him toward the door, holding back tears and biting her lip.

CHAPTER 27

When Angel and Paige finally woke up, it was almost midday. Angel went outside to investigate what Mingan was doing.

Mingan had just five adult dogs remaining and one sled, the dogs and sled which he had left behind for Abbie while they were away. Two sleds would be needed for him to get Angel and Paige back to the settlement. He spent the day making a new one. Angel watched and gave what help he could. He was so inspired by Mingan for keeping alive such skills to pass on to his son. The knowledge acquired and practiced over millennia by the indigenous peoples of North America was at risk of being lost forever. Many of them now relied on what they could buy online or at a store. He felt privileged to know someone such as Mingan.

The next day, Mingan took them back to the settlement, he on one sled with two dogs and Angel and Paige on the other pulled by the other three. They said their goodbyes. Angel was overcome with a great sense of loss watching

Mingan leave. He didn't know when, or if, he would get to see him again. Mingan had become like the elder brother Angel always wanted but had never had, someone he could have turned to for advice. There had been no father figure in his life, and his mother, while loving, hadn't been able to take the place of a male role model.

Joe put them up for the night, and the next day Maisie arrived with the same small plane they had flown in on a couple of weeks ago to fly them back to Saskatoon.

"So how was your trip?" she asked as they climbed on board.

"Great," answered Angel.

"Yeah, good thanks," added Paige.

They didn't expand further so Maisie fired up the engine and they flew back in silence. Angel didn't get the same thrill this time from the flight. His mind was preoccupied with what would happen when he made it back to Phoenix.

Back at Paige's apartment, she took a shower first and then Angel. At last, they were able to properly wash away the accumulated sweat and dirt of two weeks. As Angel stood showering, he was surprised but delighted to see Paige come back into the bathroom, let her robe drop to the floor, and join him in the shower. The sexual tension which had existed out on the trail boiled over. They held each other tight, kissing and delighting in each other's intimate caresses then moved to the bedroom where, with the passion of new lovers, they made love for most of the night.

Angel awoke feeling renewed and confident. They had crossed a huge wilderness and survived. For the first time in a long while he felt the future would be better, one which he might get to share with someone. Paige was already up cooking breakfast. He joined her in the kitchen, giving her a mischievous hug from behind.

"Well, good morning. How do you like your eggs?"

"Just as I like you, over easy."

That made them both laugh.

"When do you plan on leaving? Not that I want you to go," added Paige quickly.

"As soon as, I guess. I'd love it if you could come with me. I couldn't have done this without you."

"I would absolutely love to come along, but are you sure you want me to?"

"Of course I'm sure. I'd like nothing better."

"Okay then, let's do it. Eat while I get my things together," she said placing his breakfast on the table.

A few hours later they crossed the border back into the States, going off road as Angel had when entering Canada. That night they found a motel outside some podunk town in Montana. The following morning they were underway early, heading south. By late afternoon the day after, they'd reached the tiny town of Mexican Hat in southeastern Utah close to the Arizona state line.

They stayed in a motel above the Colorado River. It should have been in full flow with snowmelt but it wasn't. Another winter of abnormally low snowfall had come and gone, and the river had dropped to another all time low.

"We'll reach Phoenix tomorrow, get set up in a motel somewhere, and call the networks. I want to be interviewed on the steps of the Governor's office, and give him a start to his week that he won't forget," said Angel while they sat on the bed. "By the end of the day, he'll be forced to have a press conference, and I'll get my chance to confront him in person."

"We're probably going have to spend some time with a reporter first, get them onside. This whole thing is huge. They'll want to be sure of their facts before they start making allegations about the Governor. They'll be worried that they might end up looking stupid. You need to be prepared for it taking a little longer than you think. Remember, the video we had is under the ice in Canada."

"Yeah, you're right. At least I still have the emails implicating the Governor from my mom's bank deposit box. Anyway, thanks for coming along. It makes it a lot easier having you here."

"I want to do this," she replied throwing her arms around his neck and pushing him back onto the bed. "What do you say to sleeping in tomorrow?"

"Sleeping? That's not what I had in mind," he grinned.

They left the motel around ten and drove into Arizona. Angel preferred to take the backroads wherever possible. The police might still be looking for him. There was little traffic. A vehicle came the other way only occasionally, and the rear view mirror reflected nothing but empty highway. The road ran through a wide valley set between arid, ochre mountains rising abruptly on either side. Vegetation was sparse, mainly sagebrush. Angel slowed down.

"I need a break, let's pull over for ten minutes."

"We could sit by that rock right there."

Although it was only April, the temperature

had already climbed above ninety. After a few weeks in the icebox, they delighted in feeling the heat envelope their faces like a warm towel. The sun, almost white in its intensity, shone down from a cloudless sky.

Behind the rock and out of sight of the highway, they sat enjoying their break. It had been a long journey.

"Time to move on," said Angel standing up. Immediately, he crouched back down. "Stay there!" he shouted at Paige who had been about to get up.

Like a Jurassic bird of prey, a drone was flying toward their vehicle. It passed low, followed by the sound of an explosion as the missile it had released destroyed his mom's SUV. It exploded into hundreds of fragments that flew in all directions, some just missing them as they hit the ground all around them with the ferocity of large hailstones.

If they had returned to the vehicle only seconds earlier, there would now be nothing left of them but burned remains, their limbs as scattered as the pieces of the vehicle. From behind the rock, they watched orange flames and acrid smelling black smoke leap skyward from the other side of it.

Once the debris ceased raining down, they

cautiously stood up. The drone had flown on toward the horizon, becoming only a speck in the distance. It crossed Angel's mind that the hard copy emails implicating the Governor had also gone up in smoke, but right now that wasn't a priority.

"We need to get out of here. I'm sure they'll be sending someone to check they got us."

"We're in the desert miles from anywhere."

"Don't you worry about that, this is where my Apache blood comes in useful. I know how to survive out here." He took her hand. "Come on. Let's get away from the highway and head to those mountains. They'll give us cover."

Once more they moved off into the wilderness, a very different wilderness to the one they had faced in Saskatchewan. Here the enemy was heat and dehydration. There were no wolves to contend with but plenty of venomous creatures whose bite or sting could end their hike to safety.

Keeping a wary eye on the sky above them, they crossed the parched and empty valley. Neither spoke, fear had turned their mouths to sandpaper. Once again, they were the prey being hunted.

They walked quickly until they reached the mountain slopes where they could ascend out of sight behind rocks. However, they both knew that the technology being used to hunt them down was state of the art, and already government agents were probably checking the car wreckage to make sure that the strike had been successful.

CHAPTER 28

"Hi, it's Jennifer here, Jennifer Grant. Thanks for taking the call. I just wanted to let you know that we've got credible testimony from a Julia Skopoulos, an intern in the White House last year. She says the President had sex with her when she worked there. We'll be going live with the story in two days. I thought you'd like to know to give you time to reach out to me if you have any comment to make before then."

"What are you talking about?" spluttered Brad Regenhardt, the White House Press Secretary.

But she'd already hung up. He knew Jennifer well, she had a reputation as the top investigative reporter in the city, and with her name behind it the damage to the Presidential campaign from a story like this would be enormous. Today, the President was in Boston campaigning so Brad called his Chief of Staff.

"You can't see him until tomorrow. As soon as he gets back, he's gotta get across town to a fund-raiser. Half of Hollywood's gonna be there. The photo ops will be amazing. There's no way he can be late for that."

"You don't understand," insisted Brad. "He needs to know tonight. I have information that could wreck his campaign."

"You're so dramatic sometimes, Brad. Exactly what is it that could possibly be so important?"

"I'm not going to discuss it with anyone until I've briefed the President. You're going to have to trust me on this one."

"I'll see if you can talk to him while he's getting changed."

"No, that won't work. It's not something I should talk about if the First Lady is around."

"Are you shitting me?"

"Absolutely not. Why would I?"

"He's not been fooling around has he?"

"You'll find out the reason soon enough."

"I'll take that as a yes. I'll ask if he can see you briefly in the Oval Office around seven. Be there outside, waiting. I can't promise anything."

Brad was called in at seven precisely.

"This sure as hell better be important, Brad.

You're making me late for a crucial fund-raiser."

"It is Mr. President." He proceeded to explain.

"God damn it!"

"Sir, is that a denial or affirmation?"

"A denial of course! The Republicans have probably put her up to this."

Brad was concerned, the President hadn't made eye contact when he answered. He also remembered Julia, an attractive young woman, and how the President had flirted with her quite openly. Power was an aphrodisiac, and Jackson was the most powerful man in the world. It all seemed perfectly plausible. Brad coughed nervously, summoning up his courage.

"I need you to be totally straight with me on this, Mr. President. I can't do effective damage control if I don't know the truth. We don't want another Monica Lewinsky affair. President Clinton was almost ruined by that. And he wasn't seeking re-election."

"I've told you already, Brad, it's a lie. You need to get your people on this tonight, find out the dirt on her, and kill this thing. Do not let me down."

Jackson strode out of the room in a foul temper to join the glitterati of the movie world, his evening ruined.

CHAPTER 29

The only sound in their world was a solitary drip, drip. Both were reflecting on recent events. Their SUV being bombed, the helicopter attack while they hiked along an open ridge, falling into an underground lake, and the terrifying underwater swim through a narrow tunnel into another cave where they were now trapped some fifty feet beneath the surface of the earth.

Daylight tantalizingly called them from above. There was no way out. Angel and Paige were entombed, condemned to remain here for however long it would take to die if no one found them. And they would take a long time to die. Out in the desert without water dehydration would have killed them in a couple of days. Here there was water in abundance. If not found, they would die from starvation. That would be a slow and agonizing process. How ironic that water should be their purgatory in the desert. That in trying to stop a pipeline bringing water to the Southwest they were now surrounded by it.

Should they shout? Who would hear? They

were in a remote location. The chances of anyone being nearby were small, and if someone was, who would they be? The only people likely to be in the vicinity were those who were trying to kill them earlier.

A deep despair had wrapped itself around Angel. He'd traveled so far, come so close, and now they were stuck in nature's prison to rot. Paige spoke first.

"I think we should shout for help."

"So they can find us and kill us?" Angel challenged her.

"What choice do we have? Stay here and we'll die a slow and agonizing death. Wouldn't a quick ending be preferable if they intend to kill us?"

"Is that what you want?"

"I don't want to die that's what I want, and we've got a chance of living if we're found."

"Let's wait a while. Tomorrow maybe."

"Tomorrow? Anyone looking for us might be gone by then." Paige stood up, looked upward and shouted. "Help! Help!" Her voice echoed loudly around the chamber.

"Shut the hell up!"

Angel grabbed her leg but she kept on calling. He stood up and put his hand across her mouth to stop her. She bit his hand. They struggled and fell to the ground.

"I can't believe you did that," she said angrily, pulling away from him. "How dare you assault me!"

"I can't believe you would shout like that and put our lives in danger."

"Put our lives in danger? Like they aren't already."

They sat in silence, both seething with resentment toward the other. Up above them, darkness came and their shaft of downlight was lost. A few stars were visible in the small piece of night sky which they could see. Angel felt as disconnected from planet earth as those stars. He and Paige may only have been fifty feet underground, but they may as well have been thousands of light years away. There was no way of getting to the surface, no way out.

Morning came. Their bodies ached from lying on the hard rock floor.

"Well, do you still think we should keep quiet?" asked Paige accusingly.

"Shout all you want if it'll make you feel better." Angel was beyond caring.

"What's the point."

She put her head in her hands. Angel felt

guilty, she was in this predicament because he had let her come along. He should have come alone, not risk her life as well. He got up and moved over to her and put his arm around her. She leaned her head in toward him. Neither noticed the three figures descending on wires until they landed beside them. Angel's relief at being found was tempered by apprehension about what the consequences would be. The men wore military uniform and each held a gun. Angel stood up and stood in front of Paige.

"I'm the one you want. She's not part of this."

"Didn't you guys get the memo?" Paige had moved out from behind Angel. "I was bringing him back to Phoenix, so what the hell did you think you were doing trying to kill us."

"There was a temporary breakdown in communication with the CIA, ma'am," answered one of the soldiers."

Angel looked from one to the other, bewildered. "What's going on?" A sickening realization turned his stomach over like a punch to the gut. "Are you on their side? What the-"

He lurched at her but a soldier grabbed him from behind.

"You're no better than a whore," he spat out in rage.

"Hey, don't you talk to her like that," said the soldier who now had him in an arm lock.

"It's okay," said Paige. "Yes, I serve my country, and I'm proud to do so."

"I can't believe this. How could you? I trusted you."

"I was just doing my job."

"Doing your job! Was screwing me part of that too?"

"It worked. You never suspected me, did you? And a woman has just as much right to sexual pleasure as a man, though I didn't get a great deal from you."

Angel ignored the provocation. He had a greater concern.

"What about Mingan and his family? What's happened to them?"

She lowered her eyes to avoid his gaze.

"How can you live with yourself."

Angel tried to lunge at her. He wanted to kill her, she'd let the only people in the whole world he felt close to be murdered. In his fury he almost broke free, but the soldier tightened his grip.

"Time to get out of here," said one of the other soldiers. "Best if you go up first, ma'am."

She hitched herself to the wire and was winched to the surface. The soldiers and Angel followed. As he stood there handcuffed and blinking in the bright sunshine, two helicopters landed whipping up the dust and forcing him to shut his eyes. They pushed Angel into one of the helicopters. Paige climbed on board the other. They rose above the desert, hovering briefly before heading north-west.

Angel wondered how they would kill him. Would they throw him out and let him fall to his death, or take him to some remote location and shoot him? Either way no one would know what had happened to him. In death, as in life, he would be a nobody. He'd tried to make a difference like so many of his ancestors had tried but the odds stacked against them were too overwhelming.

CHAPTER 30

The Julia Skopoulos affair was receiving saturation coverage in the media. Dean Carson, the victor of the Republican primaries, and soon to be crowned as their nominee at the Republican convention in New Orleans, couldn't believe his good luck. He could just sit back, enjoy the scandal, and wait for the polls to turn in his favor.

In Washington, the President was to make a statement later that afternoon. He paced back and forth like a caged animal, waiting for Brad Regenhardt. A knock on the door signaled his arrival.

"Come in. You're late."

"I've been getting an update. I've good news, great news in fact. It turns out she's twice made sexual harassment claims. Once in a part time job she had when still in high school, and once at college. Both times the defendants fought the claims and won. She has a history. She's nothing more than a grifter."

Jackson's face lit up in a genuine smile for the first time in days. He walked over to Brad giving him the high five.

"Let's go kill this."

Across town, Julia was besieged. Her every move monitored, reporters and photographers surrounding her whenever she came outside, trying to attract her attention. If they couldn't get an answer to their shouted questions at least they could get a photo. Followed wherever she went, Julia realized now that she hadn't thought this thing through properly. If this was what victims had to endure, no wonder so few came forward. Leaving her apartment in the dead of night, she'd gone to stay at her parents' house. The media had tracked her down and were camped out twenty-four seven across the street. Julia wanted it all to end but it was too late, Pandora's box had already been opened.

The President strode quickly and confidently the short distance to the James S. Brady Press Briefing Room. Brad almost had to run to keep up.

"Sir, we haven't discussed what you'll say."

"No need to worry, Brad. I didn't get to be President by being lost for words."

"But, sir-"

The President ignored his plea and entered the room. His eager audience stood up.

"Please be seated."

They sat and waited. You could have heard a pin drop. The anticipation was evident on the face of every journalist present. He scanned the room, saying nothing and raising the drama to an even higher level of intensity.

"I know why you're all here today. You want to know if I had sex with Julia Skopoulos. I...I..."

He hesitated. They waited for his denial, but he had stopped talking and seemed lost in thought. Brad, standing to one side, wiped the sweat from his brow. He knew they should have rehearsed. The President was going to make a mess of this. It would be his undoing. After what seemed like an eternity to Brad but in reality was only a matter of seconds, the President resumed talking.

"Many women in our society are wronged. They fear speaking out about their experiences, fear that they will be ridiculed, that they will lose their jobs, and be put under severe pressure to change their testimony. It's been like that since time immemorial, but that doesn't make it right."

Frowning, Brad folded his arms to comfort himself. Exactly where was the President going with this?

"I'm not going to add to those wrongs. I'll be completely open with you. I had sex with Julia on five separate occasions." A gasp ran through the assembled journalists like a Mexican wave on steroids. "I know that I shouldn't have. I'm sorry, deeply sorry for the upset I am causing my devoted wife and family, and I say sorry to all Americans who are offended by my behavior. I want to apologize to Julia, too. Her life is now probably a living nightmare, under intense media scrutiny day and night. It's something I signed up for when I went into politics but not Julia. She is a young woman simply trying to get on with her life.

"Do my actions make me unfit to be President? That's not for me to answer but for the voters in November. I have been guilty of misjudgment. All I can say to you is that I'm a man, with a man's urges. I was flattered by her attention. I transgressed, I'm only human. I have never claimed to be anything else. I'm far from perfect and don't pretend otherwise. What I can promise you is I will always tell the truth, even though that can sometimes be the hardest thing there is to do. That is all I have to say. Thank you."

The room erupted. The journalists were all on their feet, clamoring to be noticed, desperate for the President to point at them and invite their question. He didn't. He turned and walked out.

Brad unfolded his arms. Jackson was taking a huge gamble. He only hoped it would pay off. Only time would tell but he had a sneaking suspicion that the President hadn't hurt his chances of re-election.

Less than an hour later, Julia stood on the front steps of her parents' home with her publicist to confirm the President's story. She would have her fifteen minutes of fame and make enough from talk shows and a book deal to profit. She was grateful that the President hadn't denied it and spared her months of intrusive investigation. Julia was looking forward to getting her life back, still not appreciating that she would always be known as the intern who had sex with the President.

In her office, Delores, who'd been watching the press conference on TV, slammed her hands on her desk and let out a scream of frustration. She couldn't believe her ears. The Republicans might be crowing now but she understood the voters, they would forgive him. Yes, it would hit his vote in the Bible Belt but he was never going to win there. His support was concentrated on the coasts and in the big cities where attitudes were more liberal.

History showed America loved a repentant sinner. He would pay his penance for some weeks yet, facing endless interviews on the subject. However, he would weather the hurricane of salaciousness currently sweeping across the nation.

She'd been convinced that he would deny it. A long, drawn out scandal would have finished him, led for demands for a candidate that could win, and she would have been in pole position to claim that vacancy. Delores had to give him credit, he certainly was the smartest operator she had ever met.

But everyone has their Achilles heel, even Ted. It was merely a case of finding it.

CHAPTER 31

Angel had lost count of the days. He spent them in a small cell less than eight feet by six. A small grille high up on the outside wall let in a little daylight. There was another grille at face height in the metal door, but the corridor outside was unlit so shed no light into his prison room. He had a narrow bed, a small sink, and a toilet, nothing else.

Once a day, they let him out into a dusty yard surrounded by tall walls topped with barbed wire. It was the same yard which he could see if he stood on his bed and jumped toward the grille, holding the bars for a few moments to look outside until he could hold them no longer and dropped to the floor. This was his world, not the wide open spaces he thrived in. He was trapped like a creature in a zoo.

The temperature was equivalent to a sauna. As a prisoner, there was no air conditioning for him. He'd concluded he was probably being held at a high security military base somewhere in Nevada. The helicopter had flown in that direction before they'd blindfolded him not long after takeoff. The occasional roar of jet fighters and vehicle noise were the soundtrack to his life now, the sound of human voices absent.

When he first arrived, they woke him up in the middle of the night, shining a bright light in his face and dragging him off to a windowless room for interrogation. Who else knew? What did they know? He told them time and time again that no one else knew. He wasn't going to reveal that he'd told the Apache elders at San Carlos and have their deaths on his conscience as well, but for hours they would keep asking, keep repeating the same questions, intent on wearing him down.

They promised him a TV, better food, and more time outside if he would co-operate. When he didn't, they employed electric shocks, beatings, and more. One night they took him to a different room. They strapped him in what appeared to be an electric chair and threatened to switch it on. That didn't work. Angel was happy to choose death over life imprisoned here. Over time the interrogations became less frequent. There hadn't been one for over a week now. Either they had given up or more likely decided that nobody else knew.

Angel fretted constantly about what had happened to Mingan and his family. What had they done to them? His imagination ran amuck in his confined surroundings. Had they sent in a hit squad, maybe in the dead of night? How had they covered it up? Had they burned the cabin down and left their bodies in there so it would be assumed they died in a fire? Angel was haunted day and night by these thoughts. He felt so naive to have thought he could challenge the might of the US government, as though he could have been David to their Goliath.

And Paige, how could he not have realized that she worked for the government? Clearly he hadn't used his brain. Another part of his anatomy had prevented him seeing what was now so obvious. How else would she have had the money to pay for their flight charters and have the latest night vision tech? And that environmental stuff she preached was just a load of bull, nothing but a front to help the CIA gather intelligence on those who posed a threat to the pipeline. He had certainly let himself be used, allowing her to string along so that she could identify who else was involved, even accompanying him on the trip back to Phoenix in case there were contacts waiting for him in the US.

Angel cursed he had ever trusted her. If he'd confided in only Mingan by now the world would know what was going on. Not only would his life be so very different but Mingan and his family would still be alive.

Being incarcerated was the worst thing of all, rendering Angel helpless. He'd expected they would kill him and he wished they had. At least then his spirit would have been free. To be free was in his blood, his DNA; being trapped, probably for the rest of his life, was the worst torture they could inflict upon him.

He drew upon all his mental resources to stay hopeful that something would change, that some opportunity would present itself, but that seemed little more than a fantasy. Two armed guards escorted him everywhere, and two always brought his meals.

Angel used the power of imagination to stay sane. He would focus his thoughts on being out there, hiking the desert or the pine clad mountains and sleeping under the stars. Being alone was something he could cope with. It was being kept locked up which was unbearable.

Today he sat on the bed in his cell like every other day waiting, waiting for another day to pass. Soon he would hear the entry door to the corridor open, and then the march of their footsteps on the concrete floor. They would halt outside and push his lunch through a flap at the bottom of his door. No words would be spoken.

Angel heard the door to the corridor open

and their boots resounding off the floor, filling the silence with an ugly noise. But wait... this time the sound was different. There was only one set of footsteps. Angel had long hoped and planned for such a moment during his interminable hours of solitude.

He got down on the floor, writhing and groaning. A face appeared at the metal grille.

"Hey, are you all right?"

Angel clutched his stomach and groaned some more. He heard the clunk of a key in the door. The soldier kicked it open with his leg. Entering, he removed his gun from his holster with one hand and turned slightly to put the tray of food on the floor against the wall so he could attend to Angel. Turning was his mistake. In a split second, Angel had leaped onto his back and pushed him face down onto the floor. The gun fell from the soldier's hand. Angel grabbed it. Now astride the soldier's back, Angel fired into the side of his head at point blank range.

It was gruesome. Blood flowed onto the floor. A young man was dead. Angel had never killed anyone before, and someone somewhere had lost a loved one just as he had his mother. He should have felt something but he didn't. There was no remorse. He was fighting for his survival, it was kill or be killed. They'd already tried to murder him before, and if they didn't execute him would keep him here to rot, forever.

There was a knife attached to the soldier's belt. Taking the knife, Angel cut off the top of the dead soldier's right index finger. He walked through the open door and out of his cell. It felt strange to be holding another's severed body part in his hand.

At the end of the corridor, he presented the finger tip to a control pad next to the door which sealed this area from the rest of the building. His pulse raced, would it work or would he be stuck here awaiting discovery and certain death for what he'd done?

He pushed the door. It didn't budge. Angel began sweating profusely, he had no plan B. He tried again. This time the control pad read the fingerprint and the door lock was released. Dropping the finger tip on the floor like a piece of discarded trash, Angel found himself in a long, wide corridor. At one end of it, he could see double doors and daylight beckoning him. There was no one around. Conspicuous in his orange prison suit, he hurried toward those doors. It was all or nothing, life or death.

Angel heard a noise behind him. A shiver ran down his spine and his muscles tensed. Any second he would be hit by a bullet. At least he could die with dignity. He pushed his shoulders back and walked on with conviction.

The bullet never came. He pushed through the double doors, glancing briefly behind him as he did so. A robot was moving away in the opposite direction.

Outside was a solitary vehicle, a laundry truck, its engine running. Seizing his chance, Angel lifted the flap of cloth at the back of it and jumped in. Shortly afterward it moved off and out of the base. Peeping out, he could see the site of his incarceration becoming smaller by the second. He was out. But soon someone would raise the alarm. He willed the truck to move faster.

Angel rummaged in the laundry bags to find some clothes to swap for his prison gear. The clothes smelled of stale sweat but he didn't care. He had a real chance now. The truck bumped along the dusty highway across a landscape more barren than any he had seen. Arizona was desert also but it had cacti and other plants. This place was nothing more than scrub and brown dirt, like the surface of another planet too hostile for life.

They reached a small town. Angel jumped out as the truck stopped at what was probably the only road junction. He spotted a larger truck parked down the road. The driver stood smoking by the side of it, sheltering in the shade its huge trailer cast. He looked as though he should have retired already, hunched and weary from a trucker's life.

"Hey mister, can I get a ride?" asked Angel as nonchalantly as he could muster.

"Sure you can, son. But I'm only going as far as Vegas."

"Perfect, that's where I'm going."

"Name's Vern."

"Nice to meet you, Vern. I'm Dwayne."

Vern threw what was left of his cigarette on the ground.

"Jump in."

Angel did so with gratitude. He began to believe he was going to make it as the truck pulled onto the highway.

"How did you get to this town? I'm figuring you don't live here."

"No, my last ride dropped me here."

"Are you Native American? If you don't mind me saying, you look like a picture I once saw of Geronimo."

"You mean Goyakla. Hopefully, I look a lot younger. He was already old when they took his photo. I'm half Apache. My family's ancestors rode with him."

"Wow, ain't that something," said the trucker as he screwed up his eyes against the harsh light coming through the windshield.

"So has there been any news, big news?" asked Angel.

"News?"

"Yeah, I ain't seen the news in a while. I was wondering what's happening in the world, with the election coming and all."

"Nothing much that I know of. Though turns out the President's been humping his intern. Still, it don't seem to have hurt his chances none. He's one lucky guy, even his wife's forgiven him. Mine would cut my dick off if she ever found out I'd been cheating on her."

Angel inferred from this that news about the pipeline hadn't broken while he'd been held captive. But then, why would it? Those in power were determined to do whatever it took to keep it secret.

In a few hours they saw Vegas rising out of the desert, an incongruous sight. A city in the middle of a barren landscape turning into a neon kaleidoscope of color while evening fell. It was like building a city on Mars, a place as unsuited to its surroundings as it was possible to imagine.

The traffic ahead slowed. Angel could see

flashing lights. A roadblock. They were trying to find him. The truck came to a halt behind the cars in front.

"I'll get out here, the traffic looks like it's gonna be stuck for some time. Thanks for the ride, Vern."

Angel jumped down, disappearing into the dusk. Taking a wide sweep around the roadblock, he walked into town in search of money.

Angel entered a casino filled with numerous rows of slot machines at which sat eager players, taking coins out of a plastic cup by their side as fast as their hands would let them to feed the insatiable beasts, which would occasionally show gratitude with lights shining and bells ringing while they vomited out an excess of the cash they had gorged on.

Angel walked up and down the rows looking for his victim. At the end of one he saw a coin on the floor. He bent down to pick it up, surreptitiously also removing a wallet sitting in the open purse of one of the feeders.

"Excuse me, ma'am, you've dropped this money."

The middle-aged woman barely turned to look at him to take it from his proffered hand. Her beast of a machine was in the midst of a feeding frenzy. If she just kept shoving those coins in, it might regurgitate them all and more.

Angel left the building quickly and in an alleyway checked his loot. There were cards and over two hundred dollars. He took the money and threw the wallet on the ground. Credit cards were no use to him.

He went first to a fast food joint to eat. Getting directions to the bus station, he walked along the sidewalk overflowing with America on vacation.

There was a bus leaving after midnight. Angel bought a ticket and sat in the waiting room. He congratulated himself. He'd done it, he had escaped. However, he made himself a solemn promise. He wouldn't let them capture him alive again.

As dawn forced the black night sky into retreat with streaks of advancing red and purple, the bus arrived in downtown Phoenix. Angel walked until he was far from the center. He reached a trailer park and banged on the door of one. There was no response so he knocked again. A bleary-eyed guy with long dreadlocks and several face piercings opened the door.

"Angel? What are you doing here, man? Where'd you go these past few weeks?"

"I'll tell you if you let me in."

He knew Jed from when they had worked in the same fast food joint. He also knew Jed's passion for posting 'news' stories on the internet, waiting for that day when a post of his would go viral and he would be living in Scottsdale, not a trailer which leaked when there was a rare fall of rain, and which let in dust and insects the rest of the time.

Angel told him of his adventure to Canada but didn't mention the murder of his mother. He had decided that was something for later. Angel didn't want to detract attention from getting news about the pipeline out. The media had portrayed his mother as a criminal, and he didn't want that slander to get in the way of his goal of ending construction of the pipeline. There would be time to seek justice for his mother in due course, but if the pipeline became a functioning reality it would be impossible to get it turned off.

"Man, that is unbelievable shit. What are you gonna do?" asked Jed.

"I intend to confront the Governor, in public. I was hoping you could be there videoing it all, and getting it out there for me. But before you're tempted to say yes, think about it carefully. They wanted to kill me and still do. If you get involved, they'll probably be out to kill you too."

"I don't need to think about it. This is the news story of the decade, dude. Once we get it out there, what's the point of them killing us? It won't make it secret again. They wanted you dead to keep a lid on it."

"Well, I hope you're right there. First, we need to know where we can find the asshole."

"Chill, man, and have a coffee. I'll find out."

Angel sat drinking and thinking while Jed interrogated his cell.

"He's downtown at noon, opening a new kid's playground. I bet the networks will be there. They follow him around like flies on horse shit. Are you happy to give me an interview to post before we leave just in case they do shoot you?"

"Sure, but I need your phone in return."

"No problem, I've got another."

Later Jed led him out to his hatchback. Dented and barely drivable, it got them to the city center.

Angel had long imagined this moment. Now that it was almost here, it felt different to how he had thought it would be. Yes, it would be extremely satisfying to expose the Governor and his cronies at last, but he would have given anything to have his mother back and let them do whatever the hell they wanted. He still missed her so.

Parking nearby, they walked toward the

spot where parents, kids, and the media were already gathered. Right on time, the Governor's car arrived. He emerged smiling and waving, shaking hands, and ruffling the hair of some of the children. What a total jerk, thought Angel. No, not a jerk; jerks could redeem themselves. Carlos Jimenez, the Governor couldn't, he was a criminal, a murderer.

The Governor listened attentively, nodding and smiling while the project manager thanked everyone for coming and then moved center stage to make his own speech before officially opening the playground.

"It's my great pleasure to be here this morning, and to thank all of you who have worked so tirelessly to raise money-"

"Governor," said Angel moving forward. "You probably won't know who I am and don't even care, but you will."

Carlos Jimenez moved his head back, unsettled by the interruption. The crowd turned to look at Angel.

"Hi everyone, I apologize for interrupting your ceremony, but the Governor ain't an easy guy to meet with. See our state's about to run out of water, and he and the government are building a secret pipeline to bring water down from Canada."

The crowd were dumbfounded and turned to the Governor for reassurance. Briefly he looked like a rabbit caught in headlights. The network cameras rolled. The reporters smiled, maybe their lousy assignment would be newsworthy after all. When the Governor spoke he had recovered his confidence.

"Look, son, I don't know what you're on but you're spoiling this very important day for these here people who have worked so hard to make this city a better place for our children, so please stop interrupting or leave."

A couple of security men moved toward Angel. He went right up to the cameras.

"I know it sounds crazy but it's true. Get your cameras up to Saskatchewan, up to Lake Athabasca, the eastern end, and you'll see what's going on."

The security guards tried to pull him away.

"Let go of me!"

He freed himself and walked off. The crowd and cameras watched him leave. There was nothing the guards could do but let him go. Jed followed. They could hear the Governor resuming his speech.

"Sorry about that folks. The poor guy seems a little deranged."

A reporter ran after Angel, followed by his cameraman.

"Hey, wait up. Can you come back to our studio and give an interview?"

"Sure," agreed Angel. If he remained with them, no one could kill him.

Jed rushed past. He was in a hurry to get his interview with Angel out on the internet.

Angel was driven to the studio in the back of the news van. Once they arrived, he followed them into the building.

"Could I use the bathroom first?"

"It's down the hall, on the left."

Angel didn't return. He was out of there. He had promised Jed a scoop. Jed could get his interview broadcast and make something from it. And he did. His post went viral and the media bought rights to air Angel's interview. Jed wouldn't get enough for a home in Scottsdale, but he would at least be able to buy a new car and trailer.

The networks immediately had their drones out searching. It wouldn't be too many hours until pictures of the pipeline would be beamed around the world.

CHAPTER 32

The Governor finished his speech quickly, and pleading another appointment returned to his office from where he rang the President.

"Hey Carlos, what's shakin'?"

Ted was in a jovial mood, which was rare for him these days.

"I'll tell you what's shakin', word about the pipeline's out."

"How?"

"I got ambushed by some punk today in front of the news cameras, shouting about it all. I'm sure it's only a matter of hours until the networks confirm his story. My lines are already jammed with reporters wanting a statement."

The Governor's voice sounded choked.

"There's no need to panic. We always knew this day would come. Too bad it's before the election but we've all prepared how to handle this eventuality. We've just got to stick with the plan. Tell your people the President will be making a statement later this afternoon. "

Following Jackson's instructions, Brad summoned the press to the briefing room. The President arrived looking calm and in control.

"About a year ago, I received news that water supplies in Southern California and the Southwest were under greater threat than anybody had previously realized. The data which we had been receiving was inaccurate. So much so that I was advised the whole area would run out in only a few years unless a new source of supply was obtained.

"I immediately gave the issue top priority. I deemed it necessary to deal with the problem in conditions of complete secrecy for reasons of national security. I was concerned if it became public before we had taken effective measures to deal with the threat, great harm would be done to the economy of California and the Southwest and the hard working people who live there. I was determined to avoid any panic and the damage which would result. As you can imagine if we had dealt with this in the public eye, investment in the area would have come to a halt, and the value of folks' homes and businesses would have been destroyed overnight.

"We have worked with our great friend and

ally Canada to solve the problem. For some time now we have been constructing pipelines which run from lakes in the north of Canada and through our country. It will provide the water needed to ensure the continued well-being of Southern California and the Southwest. The pipelines aren't completed yet and I had hoped to wait until they were before sharing the news for the reasons which I have already given. However, the project is well ahead of schedule, and I want to reassure you all that there will be no water crisis. We have it all under control."

The news programs gave the matter blanket coverage. Republicans again prematurely congratulated themselves that this would be the knock out blow which they'd hoped for, but as the evening wore on it became clear that most considered the President had done the right thing. They accepted his claim that going public would have risked enormous damage to the economy of California and the Southwest, which in turn would have threatened a collapse in confidence and a serious recession for the whole country.

Experts were rushed into the studios to give their opinions on whether the pipelines would work. The consensus seemed to be that it would. Jackson and his team noted with satisfaction that the polls were moving further in his favor.

North of the border, the reaction was less sanguine. Canadians interviewed on the street were opposed to the pipelines. In an emergency session of the Canadian House of Commons the following day, there was uproar. The Prime Minister was taking a beating, the charge against him led by his Minister of Foreign Affairs, Hannah Blake.

"Would the Prime Minister care to explain exactly why he thought it appropriate to allow a foreign power to requisition our natural resources without even consulting his own ministers?"

She had to shout to make herself heard above the undercurrent of sounds emanating from the other members of Parliament, heckling the Prime Minister as if drunkards in a bar.

"As the President has explained, putting it all out there in the public arena would have created panic and economic dislocation. We need to remember that the United States is our biggest trading partner. What hurts them, hurts us more. I took the decision that to say no would result in a severe recession, resulting in the loss of millions of Canadian jobs. The water in those lakes could keep the entire US going for years. But we aren't contemplating anything of the kind. All we are talking about is a short term and very limited extraction with a minimal and temporary impact on water levels."

"A short term limited extraction," scoffed Hannah Blake. "Do you really think the United States is going to spend billions of dollars on constructing pipelines to walk away from them in a few years time. And why, if the plan is to take water from Great Bear and Great Slave lakes, has absolutely no work at all been undertaken anywhere near those lakes? Nothing is happening north of Lake Athabasca. Could it be that the Americans are just going to take water from Athabasca, which is a much smaller lake, and which would be quickly damaged?"

The Prime Minister looked at a loss for words, he hadn't been aware of this. Sensing blood, she raised the stakes. "You have discredited your office and betrayed your country, sir. The time has come for you to resign. Go now before you are forced to go!"

A roar of agreement erupted not only from the opposition parties but from his own party too. By the following evening he'd resigned, and Hannah Blake had been requested by the Governor General, the King's representative in Canada, to form a government.

The day after Hannah Blake took over in Ottawa, she agreed with the other major political parties to form a government of national unity. At a news conference, she announced that she would be requesting the US Government to call an immediate halt to all pipeline construction within Canada while Parliament was consulted on what should be done.

The President met that afternoon in the White House with his advisers.

"Who the hell does this Hannah Blake think she is? I can't be seen to be doing what some Canuck chick tells me. Chip, we already have plans in place to protect our operations up there if we need to, right?"

"Yes, sir. I can have sufficient equipment up on the border within twenty-four hours of your command."

"Do it. Ann, I need you up in Ottawa to talk with her tomorrow. She needs to understand we mean no harm, but we will do whatever it takes to complete and protect the pipelines under construction."

Ann nodded unenthusiastically. She'd lost her drive since finding Ethan dead. Carrying around the secret that she had found his body and not stayed to assist the police, was proving hard to live with. It was the first thing she thought of every morning when she woke, and it was always there in her mind, tormenting her, and weighing her down with guilt.

"Mr. President," began Kim Chan, his

national security adviser, "you are aware of course that it is Congress that has the power to declare war. You must notify Congress within forty-eight hours of committing armed forces to military action, and they cannot remain there for more than sixty days without their approval."

"Is that right. Didn't you tell me that already?"

"I can't recall, sir, but-"

"Well, it's good to know you have an encyclopedia up your ass. I'll deal with Congress as and when I need to."

Chastised, Kim changed track.

"If hostilities do break out, you need to decide what to do about the one million Canadians living in the US. Interning them like we did the Japanese on the west coast in World War Two would be difficult."

"I agree, it's not practical. Homeland Security has been monitoring communications by Canadians here for the past year. There doesn't seem to be much of a problem. A few have become belligerent saying they would fight. We have them under surveillance."

"What about Canadian commercial interests?" asked Chip.

"I've already given orders for us to be

prepared to seize them if we need to but I don't expect that to be necessary. They're not going to want to prolong any conflict when they see their economy collapse if we shut the border. Eighty per cent of their foreign trade is with us. They're dependent on us." The President decided to end the meeting. "You can all go now. Chip, can you stay a minute?"

The others filed out.

"Things aren't good. I spoke with the Governors of California, Arizona, and Nevada earlier. We're facing a race against time. If we don't get those pipelines operational within a couple of weeks, there will be very serious water supply failures. Rainfall and snowmelt have been much less than we put in our forecasts. There is no back up plan. We can't waste time negotiating with Canada, or gradually ratchet up the pressure to get them to back down. Do you follow what I'm saying?"

"Absolutely, sir."

CHAPTER 33

Delores pulled over and parked. A hot, humid evening hung over the capital. The heat hit her like a wall when she got out of her air conditioned car, yet she had a spring in her step while she crossed the street.

Until yesterday, it had seemed there was nothing which she could do to stop Ted Jackson's runaway train to re-election. He'd dodged the Julia bullet, and with talk of conflict with Canada most of the nation was getting behind him. She'd been coming to terms with his seemingly assured victory, and had even begun considering a life outside politics and letting go of her dream to be President. Then she received a call.

"Hi, Delores," said a man's voice.

"Who is this?"

"You don't know me but I have some valuable information I think you'd like to have."

"Is this some kind of hoax?"

"No, absolutely not. Can you give me five

minutes of your time? It could change this election completely. It's too sensitive to discuss on the phone."

She was curious. He was probably a time waster, but she was willing to sacrifice a few minutes of her own time to confirm that.

"What's your name?"

"Brett, Brett Allen."

"Okay, I'll see you. Come to my office at-"

"I know where you are."

"Be here at five tomorrow. You'll have five minutes."

Brett Allen, she'd never heard of him. A Google search threw up nothing of use, although she realized it probably wasn't his real name.

At precisely five o'clock this afternoon, a dapper young African American in a polo shirt and chinos going by the name of Brett Allen had arrived at her office. She didn't get up to greet him or smile, nor did she ask him to take a seat.

"Well?" she asked, giving him a penetrating look of thinly disguised disdain with her dark brown eyes.

"May I sit down?"

"You may but the clock's ticking. I said five minutes only and I meant it."

"What would you say if I told you I had evidence implicating the President in murder?"

"I'd say you were either crazy or full of shit."

"Listen to this."

Taking his cell from his pocket, he laid it on her desk, and pressed play.

"Sir, we've got a serious risk of disclosure."

"What is it?"

"It's Ethan Bartinetti, the Secretary of State's lover. As you know, we've been monitoring him and her for some while now. It looks like he's about to spill the beans to that private detective working for the Republicans we informed you about."

"How do you propose to stop that?"

"We need to take him out. Just wanted to check you were cool with that, sir."

"Look, like I've always said you need to do whatever it takes. This thing is bigger than any one person. Casualties are inevitable."

Delores' heart missed a beat. That was the President's voice, she was certain of it. She sat back in her chair, considering the implications of what she'd heard. This could change everything but what was this guy's game, she wondered.

"So tell me, exactly who are you and how did you get this?" Her tone still bordered on outright hostility.

"I worked for government intelligence until I got fired recently."

"Why'd you get fired?"

"That's not important. I was at that meeting, and as you heard I recorded it."

"What's your motive? Money, I suppose?"

"No, it's not. If it was I'd have gone to the press and been a millionaire by now. I'm a Democrat through and through. I don't want this to be used so that the Republicans can win."

"So you tell me instead? What do you expect me to do about it?"

"I want a Democrat in the White House but not one with blood on his hands. We need another candidate. You."

"Me?" Delores pretended to be surprised.

"Yeah, it's no secret the President broke his promise to put you on the ticket. If he gets elected and this gets out we'll end up with Linda Hernandez as President. What a disaster that would be. I've always felt your views on things were in line. Let me send you the recording and leave it to your conscience."

She gave him her number. Having sent it to her, he got up to go.

"I wish you every success, Delores."

She remained seated, saying nothing and betraying no emotion. After he left the room, she leaned back in her chair and smiled. This was truly manna from heaven.

Now, a few hours later, she rang the doorbell to Ann's house. Her housekeeper opened the door.

"Hi, is Ann at home?"

"Are you Delores Knight?"

"That's me."

"Please step inside and wait here."

The housekeeper walked down the hall and disappeared into a room. A few moments later she re-appeared with Ann.

"Maddie, you can go now."

Ann came toward Delores, her eyes narrowed and unsmiling.

"How dare you come here! Haven't you done enough damage already. You need to go and not come back."

"Ann, I know how you must feel-"

"No, you don't. How could you? You've never been married, married for thirty years. Instead you wreck other people's marriages."

Ann fought to control her mounting anger. She loathed the woman and had resolved to have nothing whatsoever to do with her except when she couldn't avoid it at meetings in the White House. Her ex-husband's affair with Delores ended long ago, but Ann had still kicked him out of the house as soon as she'd found out about it and insisted on a divorce. Now Delores had the audacity to come to her home.

"I have some information about Ethan, about his murder that I think you should know." Ann looked startled, this wasn't a message she was expecting to hear, especially from her nemesis. "It will only take a few minutes of your time and then I'll be gone and out of your life for good."

"Follow me."

Ann led her into her private office and sat down behind her desk. She motioned to Delores to sit opposite her.

"How do you know about Ethan and me?"

"I didn't. Not until this afternoon, that is. A guy came round to my office with a recording. I have it on my phone. Listen."

An expression of shock and disbelief drained all color from Ann's face. She fought back tears while she assimilated what she'd just listened to.

"Here, take this, it's a copy of the recording. It's up to you what you do with it. I felt that you should know what happened. The only request I would make is that you don't say how you got it. I promised the young man who gave it to me not to reveal his identity. If they find out you got it from me, they'll be able to trace him from the security cameras in my office."

Delores was as ever Machiavellian, careful not to be implicated. She wanted to keep her options open until she knew exactly which way the wind was blowing.

"I can't believe it, I just can't." Ann didn't look at Delores as if talking to herself.

"I couldn't either, at first. But to have for President a man involved in the murder of one of his own citizens, that's too horrible to contemplate."

Delores observed Ann. Satisfied that she'd done enough, she stood up.

"I'll see myself out."

CHAPTER 34

Unsurprisingly, Ann slept badly. Early morning found her flying north to Ottawa once again. She knew Hannah Blake already. They were like friends, almost, often working together on diplomatic problems. They shared similar views and hit it off from the first time they'd met, even if with her slender figure and long brown hair Hannah made Ann feel much older than the ten years which separated them in age.

Ann couldn't help but smile while she thought of times they'd spent together at international gatherings, observing the alpha males indulging in their narcissistic posturing. She let out an involuntary chuckle, remembering how they laughed an evening away drinking margaritas in Cancun after a meeting when the President of Mexico tried to hit on Hannah. But Ann knew that today would be different.

Hannah was a self-made woman who'd started life in Vancouver. Majoring in politics at university there ignited her desire to follow a political career. She wanted a chance to make a difference. After all, she reasoned, men had run the world since the concept of government began and look at the mess which they'd made of it.

Ann understood that having achieved her goal of becoming Prime Minister, Hannah would be wanting to prove to her party and Canada she deserved to keep the job when their elections came around next year, and demonstrate that she was no pushover. There were many men in her party who wanted her job. Men who would want to portray her as too weak to deal with the behemoth to their south.

A limousine from the American embassy picked Ann up from the steps of the plane. News reporters jostled to get a statement from her. All they could get was video of her in the back seat as she was sped out of the airport.

Hannah, already fully installed in the Prime Minister's residence, met her in the library. She was seated and didn't get up to greet Ann. Ann ignored the discourtesy and attempted to break the ice.

"Let me congratulate you on becoming Prime Minister. It empowers women everywhere to see what you have achieved."

"Can we cut the small talk. I asked for all pipeline construction in Canada to stop and it hasn't. Do I have to send in troops to stop it by force?"

"I wouldn't recommend that."

"What choice are you giving me? Need I remind you, Canada is not the fifty-first State. You can't just come and help yourselves to our natural resources."

"I totally agree, Prime Minister. That is why we negotiated an agreement with your predecessor, which he signed and I'm sure you've read, but if not I'll be glad to supply you with a copy. Sovereign nations need to stand behind the binding commitments they have made. I understand the secrecy of the arrangement irritates you. However, the reasons for that are well known. Creating panic and economic collapse wouldn't have been in the interests of either of our two governments."

"I don't accept there was any need for secrecy about the pipelines. The fact of water supplies running out in the Southwest could have been kept under wraps. It's clear from the nation's reaction that they don't want our water exported to the United States. I will be consulting Parliament later this week and fully expect them to vote against the pipelines."

"The President is eager to negotiate an acceptable solution with you, however I should leave you in no doubt that he will not let over forty million people in our country have their lives ruined by lack of water when you have more than you could possibly ever need," countered Ann.

"This is not the 1700s, Madam Secretary. You and your government are making a grave mistake if you think the people of Canada will cave into your bullying and blackmail," fired back Hannah.

The political ping-pong continued without resolution. Ann was finding it hard to focus. Two allies might be on the verge of the unthinkable, yet always in the forefront of her mind was what she'd found out last night. Try as she might to banish such thoughts temporarily so that she could concentrate on the meeting in hand, her mind was spinning with images of Ethan being assassinated and her planned confrontation with the President later today.

Never in her wildest dreams had she imagined he would be involved in Ethan's murder. She knew that Ted Jackson was extremely keen to remain in the White House. But that he would go this far was something she still found hard to believe. Ann had wondered if the recording was a fake. Delores Knight was as ambitious as Ted, if not more so, and would do anything to get a shot at being President.

Nonetheless, Ann was satisfied that it was genuine.

The few months since Ethan's death had been difficult for her. She found a solace of sorts in drink. During the day she immersed herself in her demanding role, but in bed at night her demons taunted her. She'd failed to go to the police, failed to provide any evidence or assistance to catch his killer. All these thoughts raced around her mind on the flight back to DC.

Her stomach churned while she was driven from the airport to the White House.

"Ann." Jackson smiled and walked across the room to greet her. "How did it go, are we making progress?"

She neither smiled nor moved toward him. Instead, she stood there looking at him with barely disguised hatred.

"Why did you have Ethan murdered?" Her voice quivered with emotion.

The President emitted a guffaw of disbelief.

"What are you talking about? I think this whole crisis must be putting you under way too much stress-"

"Listen," she interrupted. She pulled her private phone from her purse and played the recording.

"I'll ask you again, why did you have Ethan killed?"

"Now look here," said Ted, the annoyance in his voice quite evident. "I don't know who gave you this but it's not true. It's just someone who wants to kill my chances of re-election. I don't deny that sounds like me but I can assure you it isn't."

Ann felt her confidence rise in response to his feeble reply.

"You think so, huh? Well, that will be for Congress to decide when they impeach you. How could you do a thing like this? Are you so crazed with power that you think you're above the law? Face it Ted, you're finished. And another thing, I'm resigning. Effective immediately."

She turned and walked toward the door.

"Not so fast. Aren't you forgetting something? Your prints are all over the gun." Ann halted. "It seems to me you're in it up to your neck. Revealing state secrets and fleeing a crime scene. A lover's quarrel that got out of hand, was that it? And what about your drinking problem? Most of Washington knows you're a lush. Do you really think people will believe you and this ridiculous accusation? They all know I'm not planning to give you a post in my next administration. Do you want your reputation destroyed, or to end up in jail? Is it a risk you're willing to take?"

Jackson sensed her resolve crumble and smiled inwardly. He'd outsmarted her. The scandal, the effect on her kids, her reputation. He was right, she knew she couldn't take the risk.

"No, I didn't think you would. Your resignation is not accepted. You will do your job and protect the interests of this country, and not let your ridiculous mid-life crisis crush on a man who was young enough to be your son interfere with that. I expect a written update on your meeting with Prime Minister Blake within the hour."

At home that evening, Ann wept bitter tears. She took a bottle of vodka from the fridge. Pouring herself a large glass, she raised it to her lips but hesitated. Letting out a cry of anguish, she threw the glass at the wall. It shattered into pieces like her life had.

CHAPTER 35

Carlos Jimenez, the Governor of Arizona, was sitting alone at his desk in his office at home. His wife had already gone to bed, and his youngest child, Carmen, and their only child still living at home, had gone to stay at a friend's house.

Most of the room was in darkness. A small lamp bathed his desk in a cozy light. Deciding to call it a day, he shut down his tablet and stood up. As he did so he felt something hard and sharp against his neck.

"Don't move or make a sound."

He froze in terror.

"Do you know who I am?" The voice was cold, its owner clearly had no compunction whether he should live or die.

"N..no," stuttered the Governor. "What is it you want? Money? It's in my desk drawer. Take it all."

"I'm not interested in money. It has no value

to me. I'm Maria Fuentes' son. Just as you had her murdered, tonight I'm going to kill you. And as you bleed to death, a cloth stuffed in your mouth so you can't scream for help, I will scalp you. Exactly as your Spanish ancestors taught us when they invaded our land."

Angel was enjoying this act of revenge. The first time he'd killed he had felt nothing, this time he would feel satisfaction.

"Please, no," begged the Governor in a constricted voice. His legs buckled with fear and an involuntary release of urine ran down his inner thigh. He tried to steady himself, laying the palms of his hands on his desk for support. "It wasn't me. I didn't have her killed. You've got to believe me".

"Who was it then?"

"I don't know, I swear."

"You're lying. Tell me who or you'll die."

Angel pressed the blade harder against the skin on the Governor's neck, grazing the surface.

"The President."

"Why should I believe you?"

"I record my calls. I save the important ones. I have them right here, on my tablet."

"Play it for me. You can sit down but don't try

anything."

Angel removed the blade from the man's neck to let him sit and then re-positioned it once he had done so. With shaking hands, the Governor switched his tablet back on and found the recording.

"Ted, we have a problem. The editor of our biggest newspaper called to say one of his journalists has been approached by my former secretary. Somehow the bitch has gotten hold of a whole bunch of information about the pipeline and the journalist wants to run with it."

"Shit."

"The good news is the editor's a friend of mine and owes me big time. He's agreed not to publish, but I'm concerned she'll go elsewhere with it."

"Did you get the name of the journalist?"

"Yeah, a Hank Dubois."

"And this former employee of yours, what's she called?"

"Maria, Maria Fuentes. What are you gonna do, Ted? The news is gonna get out."

"I'll have it taken care of, Carlos. You don't need to worry about it. Don't breathe a word to anyone about this."

Angel said nothing for a few moments while

he processed what he'd heard.

"Okay, here's what's gonna happen. You're going to video yourself here and now, say who you are and exactly what happened."

"But-"

"Do it, asshole. And remember, pull any tricks and you're history."

Removing the blade from the Governor's neck, Angel stood back.

Carlos did as required and recorded his confession. When he finished, Angel grabbed the tablet and sent a copy to his phone together with the recording of the original conversation with the President, all the while keeping a wary eye on the Governor.

"I'm leaving now but if you raise the alarm, you're never gonna see your daughter again."

"Where is she, what have you done with her?" demanded the Governor rising from his chair.

"She's unharmed but in a place no one is ever going to find her. I'll get word to you soon enough where she is. If you tell anyone about our meeting, you won't ever get her back and she'll die a horrible death from thirst. So think on that before you do anything stupid."

Angel exited through the patio windows,

disappearing into the night. The Governor touched his neck. It was sore from where Angel had pressed the blade and wet with blood. He needed to let the President know, but he couldn't. His daughter's life was at risk. Yet how could he trust the word of that half breed? He was furious the day of Maria's shooting when the cops let him get away, and even more so when he'd turned up the other day and got away yet again. That son of a bitch needed to be caught and tortured if necessary to reveal where his daughter was being held, and his phone taken before he could use it and the Governor's career was destroyed. He called security.

"I've been attacked. The intruder's in the grounds escaping right now. Make sure you take him alive and get his cell phone."

The guards sprang into action. Bright lights illuminated the entire property, turning night into day. Angel was taken by surprise. He'd watched the Governor's daughter leave earlier that evening as she shouted goodbye, saying she'd be back in the morning while he crouched behind a large cactus, waiting. He had thought his bluff about the girl would have worked. Why would the Governor risk his own daughter's life? Now Angel needed to get out of here before he was shot. He had the evidence he needed. The President and the pipeline would surely be done for now, and his mother's death wouldn't have been in vain.

Running toward the perimeter wall, Angel jumped as high as he could, managing to grab the top of it. With a massive effort of will power, he pulled himself up. He was going to make it, helped by the adrenaline rushing through his veins. Just as he got himself up there, shots rang out, immediately followed by an intense pain in his left leg.

Angel jumped down from the wall onto the sidewalk on the other side. His leg folded under him. He got up and hobbled across the street where he collapsed behind some bushes.

Hearing the guards approaching, he lay completely immobile even though his leg hurt more than the worst cramp he'd ever experienced. They were now only feet away, but they didn't see him and passed by. Getting to his feet, Angel limped away in the opposite direction.

"Don't move!"

Angel had already promised himself that he wouldn't be captured alive again. Ignoring them, he kept moving. They could go ahead and shoot him.

They didn't. The two men ran after him, jumping on him and pushing him to the ground. Dragging him back into the grounds of the

Governor's mansion, they locked him in one of the garages and left. Soon they returned with the Governor. He surveyed the scene with a grim satisfaction. Angel half lay, half sat in a back corner, blood oozing from his leg wound.

The guards gave Angel's cell to the Governor. Throwing it on the floor, he stamped on it until it broke. He smiled briefly. He'd prevented news getting out about the cover up. No longer would he need to contact the President and embarrass himself explaining how that Apache animal had nearly got the better of him once more. Now he could have this low life beaten to death if he didn't reveal exactly where his daughter was being held. The Governor had already tried calling her cell but it diverted to voicemail.

"Where is she?" he demanded.

Angel said nothing. He was prepared for death even though he expected to be tortured before he died.

"I'll ask you one last time. Where is my daughter?"

Angel didn't answer.

The Governor addressed the two security guards. "Okay, fellas, do what you need to. But make sure you find out where she is before he dies."

The moment he left, they began beating him. Angel yelled out in agony as they kicked his injured leg. He didn't know how long it lasted. At some point he passed out.

He came to when they threw a bucket of cold water over him. It won't be long until I'm dead and not hurting any longer, he told himself to give him the strength to bear the next beating. The guards moved in closer to continue but stopped when the cell of one of them rang.

"Yeah? Oh...okay. That was the Governor. It seems this asshole here was lying. The girl's just rang her mom, she's over at a friend's house. We can just leave him here to die. Let's go, he'll bleed to death from that wound soon enough. We'll dispose of the body in the morning."

They left Angel alone, locked in the garage. He lay on the concrete floor, light headed and increasingly weak from the continuing loss of blood. He didn't expect to see another dawn. Angel thought of the few people in his life who he'd really cared about: his mother, his grandmother, and Mingan. He hoped he would meet them again in the spirit world.

CHAPTER 36

It was already past eleven at night on the shores of Lake Athabasca. Although the sun had dipped below the horizon, darkness hadn't come. The light was soft, infused with the stillness and serenity that comes with evening.

Off-duty soldiers sat drinking beers and playing cards around the fire they'd built to keep away the mosquitoes, which were the bane of their lives during the short summer.

"What do you think that crack team of marines was doing here today?" asked one.

"Sent to help us, I guess. From what I heard, hostilities could break out any moment."

"You really think so? I don't like it. This ain't crazy terrorist dudes we'd be fighting. Canadians are like us."

"Our job is to obey orders, not have opinions," interrupted another. "Anyway, it's about time they had a reality check. We can't sacrifice California and the Southwest just because they won't sell their precious water to us. Most of it's under ice nine months a year, and when it ain't it flows into the Arctic Ocean where it's no use to anyone. So what's their frigging problem with the pipeline, that's what I wanna know."

"I sure as hell don't know but I need to pee," said the first.

"Watch out for the skeeters. They're one kinda cocksucker you don't want giving you a blow job," shouted another after him.

They all laughed. The soldier walked over to the wall of the pumping station. He was chilled. It was good to be drinking with his buddies and having a good time after a long day working. He'd consumed several beers and wobbled slightly, watching the liquid patterns he was creating on the wall. As he zipped, an almighty force blew him backward and off his feet. An explosion blew through the wall, hurling debris in all directions.

"Jesus Christ!" shouted one of the other soldiers. They threw themselves on the ground, putting their hands over their heads to protect themselves. As soon as the rain of rubble ended, they were up on their feet running over to the soldier who had been closest to the blast. There was nothing they could do. He was already dead, which was probably a blessing since his upper half was no longer attached to his lower body. A horrible odor, like burned meat with a noxious sweetness, came from the torso. The smell was so strong that it was almost a taste. Some of the soldiers gagged.

"Motherfuckers!" yelled one. "They're gonna pay for this."

A couple of hours later two thousand miles away in Washington, the ringing of the President's bedside phone woke him. He looked at the time and grimaced. Four in the morning.

"Yeah?" he answered stifling a yawn.

"I'm sorry to disturb you, sir, but there's been a significant development, and I thought you would want to be told immediately."

"What is it?"

"There's been an attack on our facility at Lake Athabasca. An explosion, one soldier killed and several injured."

"I'll be straight down."

He quietly got out of bed. His wife was sleeping still, she had become accustomed to night calls and they rarely disturbed her. Throwing on some casual clothes, he went downstairs. His aides were waiting outside the Oval Office.

"Who did it?" he asked, leading them in and

pouring himself some coffee.

“We don’t know, sir. It seems unlikely it would have been the Canadian military. It’s more likely to have been some eco-terrorist group.”

“Is the damage significant?’

“No, if they were hoping to knock the place out, they didn’t do a very good job.”

“I’m going upstairs to take a shower. I’ll be ten minutes. I want a call set up with the Canadian Prime Minister for when I get back.”

“We’re told the Prime Minister can’t be woken yet, sir,” said one of Jackson’s aides on his return.

“Well, that’s just not good enough. I don’t give a fuck if she’s not getting her beauty sleep. Get me her office now!”

The aide rang again. When someone answered, the President grabbed the phone from him.

“It’s the President of the United States here. I don’t want to hear any crap about not waking the Prime Minister. You need to tell her to get on the phone in five minutes or she’ll be waking up to American tanks in her backyard.”

He slammed the phone down. Those in the room with him said nothing, startled by his outburst.

"Don't just stand there, get on with what you need to do and leave me in peace!" They scurried from his office.

He ran his fingers through his hair, clenching his other hand as he did so. Ted Jackson felt so tense these days. So much was riding on getting those pipelines completed in time. The country's future, and his future. His phone rang.

"It's the Prime Minister of Canada, sir," announced a woman's voice.

"Put her through."

"I sure hope this is important," said Hannah Blake.

"You're damn right it's important. A few hours ago, your people blew up our facility at Athabasca, killing one person and injuring many others."

"I don't accept that my people did any such thing."

"Well, it's either them or some terrorists who you can't control."

"Or more likely a put up job by the United States to legitimize an invasion of Canada."

"That is a despicable falsehood. It's clear to me, Prime Minister, that even if your military didn't do this my men up there are in danger, and you aren't capable of protecting them. You and I are meeting at the UN this afternoon. I expect agreement from you at that meeting to the pipeline construction continuing and to us sending in extra troops or I'll have no choice but to send our forces over the border."

He hung up. Hannah felt powerless. The US was going to invade its neighbor, its erstwhile ally, something that would have seemed unthinkable only a few weeks ago. Was she living in some parallel universe, she asked herself. No, this was actually happening, unbelievable though it seemed.

The President called his Secretary of Defense.

"Chip, I'm giving the order to invade first thing tomorrow if the Canadians don't come to their senses today. Make sure everything is ready."

"Yes, sir. I'll call a meeting with the Joint Chiefs immediately."

In Ottawa, Hannah met with her advisers. No one spoke other than her. They looked at her, wanting an answer, a solution. Something to stop this roller coaster to armed conflict which Canada had no chance of winning. Her instinct told her that she'd been right when she accused the President of organizing the attack but now he had what he needed, something with which to justify his actions.

"I need a meeting of the Cabinet, here at eight." She departed, shoulders slumped. Her steely determination of recent days had vanished and she looked beaten.

CHAPTER 37

Throughout the day, US forces continued to amass at strategic locations near the Canadian border, and at the planned entry points into Saskatchewan in particular. Opposite them was the Canadian contingent. Along the border, each currently remaining within their own airspace flew fighter jets of the two countries' air forces, at times separated by little more than the twenty-foot width of the no-touch zone. Young pilots with the same hopes and dreams caught the most fleeting of glimpses of each other, someone they might soon be ordered to shoot down.

When the Canadian commander in Saskatchewan zoomed in for a closer look with his headset at the US military positions across the border, he was struck by the small number of personnel he could see. They didn't appear to have the manpower to mount a proper attack. But then he remembered, the US already utilized remotely controlled tanks and armored vehicles, and those odd looking soldiers he thought he had seen with the naked eye were robots. America no longer had to risk significant casualties, it could largely fight a war from the comfort of a control room in Nebraska. And, not visible to him, a swarm of drones were nearby, like killer bees ready to leave the hive.

They didn't know it yet, but Canadian troops were surrounded. The US had already dropped by parachute collapsible, remotely controlled artillery launchers. Now camouflaged and flat on the ground, when activated they would rise and unleash their considerable firepower from behind Canadian lines.

This would also be a cyber war. A large part of Canada's military hardware came from America, and microchips embedded in the equipment when it was manufactured could be used to incapacitate Canadian forces if hostilities commenced. For over a year now, a top secret unit in the Pentagon had been hacking into Canada's infrastructure computer systems, leaving trojans which they could activate when needed.

Belatedly, the Canadians had realized their vulnerability and were frantically working on neutralizing these threats, even releasing cyber criminals from jail to assist, but so far they had only scratched the surface of the problem. Like an enemy within, US technology was already in position and primed to cause crippling chaos across Canada.

In Ottawa, the Chief of the Defense Staff met with the Prime Minister and her Cabinet. He advised her defeat for Canada would be inevitable if fighting broke out, and significant loss of Canadian life a certainty.

The troubles of the office which she had craved for so long bore down on her remorselessly. What real choice did she now have other than to persuade her government to give in and accept the inevitable? Many countries might be secretly rooting for Canada, but none other than Russia, China, and a few rogue states, were going to endanger their relationship with the US and take sides.

At the end of the day, it all came down to money and power, and on both counts Canada couldn't hold a candle to the world's largest military and economic power. Hannah Blake would seek some vacuous communiqué to be issued by the two governments. How taking water from Canada was only a short-term measure, though she knew it wouldn't be. If you come home and find a grizzly bear in your kitchen going through your food, you back off and let it take what it wants. It's the way the world works. After all, Canada, like America, had been created by taking land from the indigenous people who were there first, so what moral high ground could the Canadians really claim now that a more powerful nation wanted some of its water?

That afternoon in New York, the President stood by the window in a room high up in the United Nations building looking over the East River below. He turned to face his advisers seated on the far side of a long conference table. The side nearest him remained unoccupied, awaiting the arrival of the Canadian delegation.

"Damn that woman!" he said venting his frustration. "It's already a quarter till three. How dare she be late. I'm inclined to send our army over the border right now and teach her a lesson she won't forget."

"Sir, we're told there was a technical issue with her airplane in Ottawa, and it's taken a little while to get a replacement ready. They should be here any minute," explained one of his aides.

"I would counsel patience, Mr. President. Hopefully, it will avoid a war and loss of life," said Ann.

Remaining in her post, Ann loathed herself for her lack of courage. She now had a highly formal, distant relationship with Ted, born out of the necessity of having still to work for a boss who she utterly loathed and despised.

"Ten minutes and no longer. If she's coming here to agree our demands, she can confirm that by phone wherever she is."

The President took his seat in the middle of everyone and next to Ann. She recoiled as though he were a nasty smell and shuffled her chair farther away from him. Shortly afterward, the door opened and into the meeting room came Hannah and her Minister of Foreign Affairs accompanied by three officials. They took their seats opposite the President and his entourage.

"I apologize for being late, there was a malfunction with-"

"We know," interrupted the President. "Anyway, you're here now and we need an answer. What's your decision?"

"We resolved in Cabinet this morning to accept what you want-"

"I'm very pleased to hear that."

The President smiled, avoiding conflict was the best outcome for him. If fighting began, he would no longer have control over events. Should things not go as planned, public backing for his stance could quickly evaporate and eliminate his current lead in the polls. He understood a war is easy to start but not so easy to end.

"I should be grateful, Mr. President, if you would do me the courtesy of allowing me to finish what I have to say."

"I'm sorry."

The President's apology was insincere. However, he could afford to let her have the self-serving rant that would doubtless be coming his way with a request for a communiqué to put Canada's capitulation in the best possible light. His team already had a draft ready for such an outcome. She began speaking again but he wasn't paying much attention. His aides could take over from here. Her voice sounded far away; he was thinking of the adulation awaiting him for solving the water shortage and avoiding a war with Canada. Jackson would be seen as a hero, his re-election assured.

"As I said, we resolved in Cabinet this morning to accept the situation, but isn't it strange how these things play out. I've since come into possession of information which I believe is a game changer."

A game changer? The words interrupted the President's daydreaming abruptly.

"Look, if you've come here to mess with me, you're wasting your time and leave me with no alternative. Our forces are ready to move at a moment's notice and you better believe it." The

President's words were loud and angry.

"I certainly do believe it, but indulge me for a moment," she responded. "We're going to play something for you. I recommend you listen carefully. I think it will have a significant bearing on the matter at hand."

One of her aides projected a screenless display in the space between them. The face of the Governor of Arizona appeared.

"I'm Carlos Jimenez, Governor of Arizona. Earlier this year, I found out my executive assistant had gotten access to my secret files. She found out about the pipelines being constructed to bring water down from Canada and contacted a journalist about it. I called the President to inform him. He wanted to keep the pipelines secret for as long as possible. He asked who they were and I told him, Maria Fuentes and Hank Dubois. He said he would have it taken care of, and told me to say nothing to nobody. Both of them were killed shortly afterward."

"Oh, please," said the President. "You surely don't expect us to fall for this. Any nerd could produce something like that, or if not, it's been obtained under duress with a gun held to his head."

"Really? Well, why don't you listen to the call between you both that the Governor recorded.

Her aide played it. "Don't tell me you're going to deny that's you and him."

"This is preposterous! Our meeting is over and you've just got yourself a war."

"I hope not. What you've just seen is being released to the media as we speak. I don't know you'll have as much support for your actions once the American people know that you had your own citizens murdered."

Jackson got up to leave.

"I'm going back to DC. Come on, let's move it," he commanded his team.

They all filed out of the room after him, all of them except for Ann who remained seated.

"May I ask how you obtained this information?"

"It was given to me two hours ago, that's why we were late. Apparently, the recording was handed in to our Consulate in Los Angeles earlier today. The guy who left it said a brave young man had given his life to get it to us. That's all we know."

"Another innocent life lost." Ann sighed, gathered her papers and walked from the room as though the weight of the world was on her shoulders.

The President's motorcade had already

departed for the heliport on East 34th Street to deliver him to Marine One, the Presidential helicopter, for the trip back to the White House.

CHAPTER 38

Less than two hours later, the President was in the Oval Office, circling his desk in a restless manner. The networks were consumed with news of the killing of Hank Dubois and Maria Fuentes. His Chief of Staff and the White House Press Secretary stood watching the TV.

"It was a legitimate and necessary thing to do," insisted Jackson. "A matter of utmost national security was at stake."

"Sir, the Republicans are saying it's government-sanctioned murder of our own citizens and are calling for impeachment," said his Chief of Staff.

"That's a diversion. My priority is to secure our nation's water supplies. Tomorrow, I'll be giving orders for the invasion of Canada. I want you back here at eight this evening-"

Their attention was again caught by the TV. "Some breaking news just coming in. We are getting reports that water supplies in large parts of Southern California and the Southwest have failed."

For a moment, there was silence in the room. Jackson wiped his hand across his forehead. He felt hot, dizzy almost. The other two stood there, staring at him.

"Don't just stand there, gawking," the President lambasted them. "You have urgent work to do."

When they'd gone, the President slumped into his chair listening to the unfolding crisis. So little water now remained it wasn't enough to keep supplies flowing. In many towns and cities, faucets had stopped functioning and toilets couldn't be flushed. The authorities had called for calm, but panic was already breaking out with fights in supermarkets as crowds of people descended on them to strip the shelves of bottled water. Slowly but surely orderly society was beginning to disintegrate.

That evening, the President met with advisors and declared a state of emergency across Southern California, Nevada, and Arizona. The National Guard was mobilized to drive water tankers to the affected areas but it was only a drop in the ocean of desert. Those who lived there understood all too well the seriousness of the situation, that water couldn't be trucked in for millions. Businesses would grind to a halt and have to lay off their workers, and soon there wouldn't be enough drinking water for people and their families.

Within hours, thousands across the region were piling their belongings into their vehicles and heading north and east to find a land where they could survive. During the following days, millions would follow their example. Traffic out of the major cities became backed up for miles. Hospitals and nursing homes were forced to evacuate their patients, and inmates in the prisons were transferred, many escaping in the confusion. Just as many thousands had migrated to California during the Depression and dustbowl of the 1930s, millions were being forced to leave the desert which they had made bloom. Bloom so well that they'd forgotten they lived in a desert incapable of sustaining that many people. Like too many straws in a glass, they had drained it dry.

The rest of America watched transfixed and horrified, shocked by how something that had seemed so permanent, which had been such a statement of modern man's omnipotence, could unravel so quickly. With the consequent failure of hydroelectric power, lights were literally going out across the Southwest.

In the space of twenty-four hours, the area had gone from success story to looming catastrophe, and the President's fortunes were ebbing just as quickly. He had taken a gamble, a gamble with the lives and prosperity of his fellow countrymen and women, the most reckless gamble in recent history. Each time the stakes were raised, he increased his bet, and now he had bet all he could and lost. While water supplies had fallen ever lower, he'd leaned heavily on the Governors not to introduce emergency rationing. Completion of the pipelines was now only a few weeks away, he assured them. He had persuaded them to continue releasing false data to hide the true picture, not willing to do anything that might compromise his chances of re-election.

The President's troubles didn't end there. Governor Jimenez of Arizona had given a press conference, confirming that what he had said in the video was true. He was focused on protecting his own skin. The man claimed he had no idea that people would actually be killed to maintain the cover up. Jackson's closest allies were quickly deserting him in droves, the asset he had once been upended and transformed into a serious liability.

Ann too had now gone on TV to talk about Ethan's murder, and how the President had threatened her if she tried to do anything about it.

Ted Jackson couldn't quite believe how fast

things were falling apart. Yesterday, he strode the world stage like a colossus. He seemed assured of re-election, and most of the nation supported his stance that Canada must provide the water which California and the Southwest needed. Tonight, he was an outcast, a pariah.

Who was that 'brave young man' who gave his life to get the news out, he wondered. It could only have been Maria Fuentes' son. He bitterly regretted his change of heart to have him interrogated and incarcerated. If only he'd had him pushed out of the helicopter when captured as originally planned, the killing of Maria Fuentes and Hank Dubois wouldn't have come to light, and Ann wouldn't have been emboldened to reveal what she knew about Ethan's murder.

Jackson didn't go to bed that night. He stayed in the Oval Office alone, downing several glasses of bourbon. Around five in the morning, he fell asleep for a couple of hours on one of the sofas.

Waking confused and disoriented, he forgot where he was. Was he dreaming? He would soon wake up next to his wife and everything would be all right. But the disaster that was yesterday came flooding back to him. He gave orders not to be disturbed.

He switched on the TV, hoping against hope that something would have changed. It hadn't. The apocalyptic images of the beginning of a mass exodus from southern California and the Southwest were being played and re-played. Scenes of uncontrolled fires were also being broadcast. With fire hydrants no longer functioning, hundreds of fires were raging across the region, far too many for the authorities to cope with. As well as accidental fires, arsonists had taken advantage of the situation to deliberately start wildfires, which were spreading rapidly in the parched conditions. The late night sky - it was still dark out West - was red and orange. Flames revealed black clouds of smoke as the news station aired video of heavy traffic leaving Phoenix. It was as though the city was erupting like a volcano.

Stock markets around the world had nosedived. From Tokyo to London, prices had been in freefall until trading had been temporarily suspended. Wall Street would open soon and a bloodbath was predicted. The millions being forced from their homes had no jobs to go to and little money. Their homes had become worthless overnight. It was the biggest economic challenge ever faced by the country, claimed news reporters.

The President understood he was finished. His disgrace would be total, his ignominy merciless. Many in his own party had already come out to join the Republicans in demanding his impeachment. He knew the math, it would happen. Jackson thought of the shame, the ridicule. A long public trial, a daily humiliation in front of the entire world, then a life behind bars. His wife, his children, his elderly parents, all so proud of him until only yesterday, and now traumatized by what he'd done.

He thought of late last night when his wife visited him, her eyes red from crying.

"Well Ted, is it true?"

He remained seated, avoiding her gaze and unable to give a satisfactory answer.

"I'm your wife. Answer me, I need to know."

He put hid his head in his hands.

"Oh my God, it's true. Were any more people killed in the cover-up?"

"Some," he said, his voice uncharacteristically meek.

"Some? Like ten, a hundred?"

"Twenty to thirty maybe. I was defending our country, it's my job. Being President is about making choices, difficult choices for the greater good. We had to keep the pipeline confidential to try and save the Southwest. You saw how the Canadian public reacted when the news got out. Yes, the loss of any life is regrettable, but should only a few people have been allowed to threaten the lives of millions?"

"The murder of American citizens is not your job. You should have handled the water crisis out in the open. I don't buy it, Ted, and nor will the folks out there."

"You don't understand."

"Oh, I think I do." Her resolve hardened. "You were willing to do anything to win, regardless of the cost. Didn't you ever think about me and the kids in all this? They've both been on the phone in tears. They looked up to you. Now they have to face the awful truth. Their own father had people murdered. Think of the damage you've done to them. And me. You're not the man I married. Power has changed you, it's made you crazy, Ted. I could forgive your fooling around with that intern but not murder. I'm moving out first thing tomorrow, and I want a divorce."

Another body blow. He sat there motionless, lost for words. His wife said nothing more either but gave him a look of contempt that crushed him.

It was now past nine in the morning. Jackson knew he wouldn't be able to hold off seeing people much longer. He went and stood by the windows. He wasn't looking through them. He was already in a prison, a prison of despair. Tears began to run down his face. How could it all have come to this? He'd entered politics with such noble intentions, but success and power had fatally compromised his judgment. Being the most powerful person in the world had misled him into thinking he was invincible.

Jackson knew what he must do. He went over to his desk and sat down, the desk from where he governed America. He opened a drawer to the right of his chair. He didn't look. He stared straight ahead, his eyes wide open not focusing on anything. He felt it and pulled it out of the drawer, lifting it toward his face. The metal was cold inside his mouth.

Four US Presidents have been assassinated. Edward Jackson was the first to commit suicide.

CHAPTER 39

Five months later in Washington on a cold, rainy January day, Delores Knight was sworn in as the first female African-American President of the United States. Not party to the water crisis debacle, she had been the perfect candidate for the Democrats. Linda Hernandez, Ted Jackson's running mate, was tainted by association even though she denied quite truthfully any knowledge of what had gone on.

Delores soothed a nation in shock. Shock at a Presidential suicide, and shock at the hollowing out of California and the Southwest. She beat her Republican rival, Dean Carson, by a comfortable margin.

Peace with Canada had been maintained. The mass exodus of people from California and the Southwest solved the immediate need for more water. However, the world's economy had fallen into a deep recession, exactly as Ted Jackson predicted it would. The cost of re-housing the millions forced to leave, most of whom remained unemployed, was huge and would probably take a generation to deal with.

In December, the earth, as if in a warning to man not to return, had inflicted a massive earthquake on the largely deserted city of Los Angeles. Large areas of it lay in ruins, eviscerated as though taken out by a nuclear attack. Had the city still been populated the loss of life would have been significant, so as with every cloud there was a silver lining. Like most cities in the region, drifters and opportunists moved into some of the abandoned homes but largely the whole area was empty and abandoned.

Delores stood in front of the US Capitol, looking at the vast crowds below her on the National Mall and beyond to the Washington Monument and Lincoln Memorial. It was in many ways a somber day. She thought of Ted, her mentor. He had the right idea but in the execution of it, he lost his way with disastrous consequences.

"America has witnessed what happens when you ignore the limits of mother nature," she said in her inaugural speech. "Southern California and the Southwest will be open to repopulation once suitable water supplies are in place. We will construct a series of desalination plants along the Californian coast, but growth will need to be limited to what the available resources can support. Agreement will be sought from Canada to obtaining water for the Great Plains. That region is fast exhausting its supply from overuse of the Ogallala Aquifer, threatening America's ability to feed itself."

The crowds listened in silence but with understanding. She concluded her speech.

"America has never run away from a challenge. We stay and do the right thing, no matter how hard that might be. That's what makes this country what it is. If we work together as one we will succeed. God bless all of you, and God bless our great nation."

Two thousand miles away, it was a warm and sunny day in southeastern Arizona. A vehicle pulled up at the general store on the San Carlos reservation. Outsiders were a rare event these days, the tourists long gone. The lake which once attracted fisherman remained empty, an expanse of hard-baked mud.

A man stepped down from his truck and went inside the store. He returned from making his inquiries, and drove off road for a mile or so leaving a cloud of dust behind him. He halted near a trailer which stood alone on a slight rise, surrounded by the ochre colored earth. Leaving his vehicle, the man walked toward the trailer, his shadow long in the early morning sun. He knocked firmly on the door.

A man opened it and looked at him. A look of shock came over him and for a moment he was speechless. His expression quickly changed, his face erupting with joy as it sank in who was standing in front of him.

"Mingan!"

"Angel."

"I can't believe it."

The two men embraced. Abbie and Wematin joined them.

"I thought you were dead," exclaimed Angel, his face still alight with happiness.

"We thought you were too."

"Hey, Jacali, come see who it is."

A young woman with long dark hair came to the door.

"Jacali, meet Mingan, Abbie, and Wematin."

"It's so great to meet you and to know you're all right. I've heard so much about you. Can I get you something to drink? I hope water's okay, that's all we have."

"Well, at least you still have some," laughed Abbie.

"Did you want to come in or sit in the sun?"

"Sit in the sun and feel the warmth. We don't

get winters like this in Saskatchewan as Angel could tell you."

Angel, Mingan, and Abbie sat down on the warm earth while Wematin ran around kicking a ball. Jacali arrived with glasses of water on a tray.

"Tell us what happened," said Angel. "I've felt so bad for so long. I was convinced you'd all been murdered. It urned out Paige worked for the government. She was a CIA agent."

"Just as well we did what we did then," said Mingan. "Once you guys left, I figured we'd better move. I was worried if you got into trouble they might come after us so I started building a new place a few miles away. I made the family live in a tent until it was ready. Not many days after you left, we saw smoke coming from the lake we used to live beside so I went over to take a look. Our cabin had been destroyed. It looked like it had been hit by a missile. A bunch of burned out wood was all that was left of it."

"I'm so sorry."

"There's no need to be. As you can see, we're alive and well."

"I got captured by the army. That was when I found out who Paige really was. I asked what had become of you but didn't get an answer so I feared the worst."

"And then what happened? We heard about the Governor's confession. The Canadian government put out a story that some young man had died getting it to them. We were worried that might be you."

"Yeah, I thought I would die. The night I got him to confess, I told him I'd kidnapped his daughter, and if he raised the alarm he'd never see her again. I figured that would give me time to get away. But he went right ahead and called security. I got shot in the leg trying to escape. The guards dragged me back to the Governor's mansion and kept me in his garage. They beat me up pretty bad.

"The Governor was mighty pleased with himself that night, getting his hands on my cell phone. He thought he was in the clear. What he didn't know was that I'd already sent the video before the security guards got to me. I sent it to a friend, Jed, who delivered it in person to the Canadian consulate in LA. Anyway, in the end they just left me there, locked up. I was losing a lot of blood from the gunshot wound, but I was able to make a tourniquet from my headband and stop the bleeding.

"Then the news must have broken because the next day I heard the cops come round. When they'd gone, the guards drove me to the hospital. They were about to evacuate the patients but I managed to get treated. The Governor must have decided it wasn't worth killing me once the news got out. He never got charged but at least he ain't the Governor no more. Though there ain't much to be Governor of now, that's for sure."

"Well, we're just glad you're safe," said Abbie.

"How come you tracked me down?" asked Angel.

"We wanted to find out what had happened to you so we hired a truck and drove down. We came here because we reckoned if you were still alive this is where you would have come," said Mingan.

"You guessed right. This is where I want to make my new life. Are you able to stay a while? I'd love the chance to show you my country."

"Absolutely, we brought a tent. We'd like to experience a winter where we're not freezing our asses off for once."

They all laughed, a laugh which reminded them how good it was to be alive and in the company of friends who they had thought they would never see again.

++++++++++++++++++++++

ALSO BY DAVID CANFORD

2045 The Last Resort

In 2045 those who lost their jobs to robots are taken care of in resorts where life is an endless vacation. For those still in work, the American dream has never been better. But is all quite as perfect as it seems?

The Shadows of Seville

A gripping and moving story of loss and love, of hatred and passion, and of horror and hope, set in Spain's most evocative city during the turmoil of the Spanish Civil War and the following decades. Lose yourself in vibrant 'Sevilla' where the shadows of the past are around every corner.

Puppets of Prague

Can the dream of freedom overcome fear and oppression? Friendships are tested to the limit in this saga spanning Prague's tumultuous 20th century. In the summer of 1914 young love beckons and the future seems bright for three close friends, but momentous events throw into stark relief the differences between them that had never mattered before.

Betrayal in Venice

Sent to Venice on a secret mission against the Nazis, a soldier finds his life unexpectedly altered when he saves a young woman at the end of World War Two. Discovering the truth many years later, Glen Butler's reaction to it betrays the one he loves most.

A Good Nazi? The Lies We Keep

Growing up in 1930s Germany two boys, one Catholic

and one Jewish, become close friends. After Hitler seizes power, their lives are changed forever. When World War 2 comes, will they help each other, or will secrets from their teenage years make them enemies?

Kurt's War

Kurt is an English evacuee with a difference. His father is a Nazi. As Kurt grows into an adult and is forced to pretend that he is someone he isn't for his own protection, will he survive in the hostile world in which he must live? And with his enemies closing in, will even the woman he loves believe who he really is?

A Heart Left Behind

New Yorker, Orla, finds herself trapped in a web of secret love, blackmail and espionage in the build up to WW2. Moving to Berlin and hoping to escape her past, she is forced to undertake a task that will cost not only her own life but also that of her son if she fails.

Going Big or Small

British humour collides with European culture in this tale of 'it's never too late'. Retiree, Frank, gets more adventure than he bargained for when he sets off across 1980s Europe hoping to shake up his mundane life. Falling in love with a woman and Italy has unexpected consequences.

The Throwback - The Girl who wasn't wanted

A baby's birth on a South Carolina plantation

threatens to cause a scandal, but the funeral of mother and child seems to ensure that the truth will never be known. A family saga of hatred, revenge, forbidden love, overcoming hardship and helping others.

Bound Bayou

A young teacher from England achieves a dream when he gets the chance to work for a year in the United States, but 1950s Mississippi is not the America he has seen on the movie screens at home. When his independent spirit collides with the rules of life in the Deep South, he sets off a chain of events he can't control.

Sea Snakes and Cannibals

A travelogue of visits to islands around the world, including remote Fijian islands, Corsica, islands in the Sea of Cortez, Mexico, and the Greek islands.

THANK YOU

I hope you enjoyed reading When the Water Runs Out. I would appreciate it if you could spare a few moments to post a review on Amazon. It only need be a few words.

Thanks so much,

David Canford

ABOUT THE AUTHOR

David started writing stories for his grandmother as a young boy. They usually involved someone being eaten by a monster of the deep, with his grandmother often the hapless victim.

Years later as chair lady of her local Women's Institute, David's account of spending three days on a Greyhound bus crossing the United States from the west coast to the east coast apparently saved the day when the speaker she had booked didn't show up.

David's life got busy after university and he stopped writing until the bug got him again recently.

As an indie author himself, David likes discovering the wealth of great talent which is now so easily accessible. A keen traveller, he can find a book on travel particularly hard to resist.

He enjoys writing about both the past and what might happen to us in the future.

Cambridge University educated, his previous jobs include working as a mover in Canada and a sandblaster in the Rolls Royce aircraft engine factory.

David works as a lawyer during the day. He has three daughters and lives on the south coast of England with his wife and their dog.

A lover of both the great outdoors and the man-made world, he is equally happy kayaking, hiking a trail or wandering around a city absorbing its culture.

You can contact him at David.Canford@hotmail.com

Printed in Great Britain
by Amazon

60354766R00180